MW00910047

MISS DEMPSEY'S SCHOOL FOR GUNSLINGERS

Other books by I.J. Parnham:

The Finest Frontier Town in the West
The Legend of Shamus McGinty's Gold

MISS DEMPSEY'S SCHOOL FOR GUNSLINGERS

•

I.J. Parnham

AVALON BOOKS
NEW YORK

© Copyright 2004 by I.J. Parnham
Library of Congress Catalog Card Number: 2004093956
ISBN 0-8034-9690-7
Published by Thomas Bouregy & Co., Inc.
160 Madison Avenue, New York, NY 10016

PRINTED IN THE UNITED STATES OF AMERICA
ON ACID-FREE PAPER
BY HADDON CRAFTSMEN, BLOOMSBURG, PENNSYLVANIA

Chapter One

Bob's first blow knocked Snide Patterson to his knees.

Some of the enthusiastic onlookers urged Bob to hit Snide again, others demanded that Snide get up and fight, and the rest called for the remaining people in Warty Bill's to come outside and watch the fun.

"Reckon you should stay down," Bob shouted as he flexed his fist. "Now that we all know who cheated on that last hand."

Snide pressed his forehead flat to the dirt and clutched his belly. Then he surged to his feet with a mighty roar.

"That's fightin' talk," he muttered.

Bob raised his hands, not in fear of a blow from Snide, but in surprise at seeing the Colt clutched in Snide's right hand.

"A five dollar pot was big enough to knock you

1

down for your cheating." Bob backed a pace. "But you got no reason to pull a gun on me."

"You called me a cheat, and I ain't." Snide raised his gun hand an inch and spat on the ground. "So we got to sort this out."

"If you insist." Bob blew on his fingers, then lowered his right hand until the fingers dangled beside his holster. "Let's sort this out."

"You ain't sorting anything out," a man said from outside the circle of onlookers.

Bob and Snide glanced to the side as the circle broke and this man strode through. He was tall and stocky and packed a Colt Peacemaker, but the gleaming star on his chest grabbed their attention first.

"This has nothing to do with you," Bob muttered.

The lawman glared at Bob. "Snide knows me well, but you're new in town. So for your information, the name's Randolph McDougal, Sheriff of Destiny. And it has everything to do with me."

Bob nodded, then lowered his head and relaxed his gun hand.

"But he said I was a cheat," Snide whined.

"Then he ain't as stupid as you look." Randolph smiled. "But you know my rules. I let you sort out your differences peacefully, or even with the occasional fist, but I draw the line at bullets. So holster the gun."

"Or what?"

Randolph took three long paces to stand toe to toe with Snide. With his left hand, he grabbed Snide's gun arm, swung the arm up, and prized the gun from his hand.

As Randolph pushed Snide back a pace, Bob tipped his hat to Randolph, then sauntered into Warty Bill's.

The onlookers disbanded, shaking their heads and muttering about the disappointing end to a promising fight, and filed after him into the saloon.

Randolph watched each man leave until he and Snide were alone on the road, then turned back to Snide.

"As you pulled a gun on that man, you get arrested—again." Randolph sighed. "And even an idiot as big as you should know what to do by now."

"I reckon as you're right." Snide thrust his hands above his head, turned, and swaggered towards the sheriff's office.

Randolph followed two paces behind until they reached the edge of town. As Destiny had few standing buildings, he had commandeered a shack beside Adam's hotel for a sheriff's office and jail. For the last three months he'd devoted most of his limited free time to shoring up the shack and adding a cell using rubble left over after the collapse of the hotel's second floor.

Snide chuckled as he pushed open the office door.

"Cell's coming along, Sheriff. You got two walls now."

"And the cell would come along a whole lot faster if I didn't waste so much time arresting troublemakers every day." Randolph followed Snide inside. "But as soon as I've finished it, you'll spend plenty of time in there."

Randolph pushed Snide towards the crate sitting at the back of the half-built cell.

Snide slid to a halt, glancing at the cell's two completed walls, then at the two-foot high third wall. His eyes traced the outline of the non-existent cell bars. He licked his lips and sat on the crate. With a wide grin threatening to consume his face, he leaned against the back wall and locked his hands behind his head.

Randolph pulled his hat low and threw Snide's gun on his desk.

"I can't stay to guard you. I got a town meeting to attend." Randolph glanced at the short third wall. "I'm trusting you to stay. Make sure you're here when I return."

Snide glanced at the short wall and gibbered to himself.

"Trust me, Sheriff."

Randolph snorted and sauntered toward the road. On the boardwalk he stood a moment, listening to Snide clamber over the cell wall, grab his gun, and clatter through the office's back window. He then continued down the road past Adam's hotel, Warty Bill's, Mrs. Simpson's parlor, and into the school, the nearest Destiny had to a large official building.

Inside, Mayor Fergal O'Brien sat at a table, which faced the door and five rows of chairs, fingering a roll of paper. Only two of Destiny's citizens occupied those chairs—Adam Thornton, the hotel owner, and

Miss Dempsey, the teacher. Both were staring at Fergal with their arms folded.

Randolph sat beside Fergal. Randolph used to be Fergal's bodyguard when he'd sold tonic, but when they'd decided that the approaching railroad heralded boom times in Destiny, they'd sought a new life as mayor and sheriff.

Fergal nodded to Randolph, then stood and threw his thin arms wide revealing his bright green waist-coat.

"Welcome, welcome, welcome, good citizens of Destiny," he proclaimed. "Unless anyone reckons some more good citizens might come."

Randolph leaned to Fergal. "Reckon all the good citizens *have* come."

Fergal sighed. "In that case, I'll open the inaugural Destiny town meeting. And I must use this opportunity to officially announce a sad event. I'm resigning as mayor."

Adam grinned. Miss Dempsey covered a yawn.

Fergal lifted his hands. "Please don't try to talk me out of it. My decision is final."

"I ain't," Adam murmured, joining Miss Dempsey in the yawning.

"I suppose I'm sorry to see you go," Miss Dempsey said.

"I'm still staying in Destiny. I'm opening a shop and selling my universal remedy to cure all ills."

Adam chuckled. "Good. Those rats are returning to my hotel. Need something to kill them."

"My product is genuine," Fergal snapped. He

tucked his thumbs into his waistcoat and puffed his chest. "Only thing you need to wonder is how many people I will cure."

"Only thing I wonder about is when you are resigning as mayor."

"Copies of my official announcement will grace every building in town." Fergal unfurled the roll of paper and read from it. "All nominations to be the new mayor of the finest frontier town in the West must be entered by sunset Wednesday. If more than one candidate applies, the election's to be held in seven days on Saturday."

"All right." Adam slapped his legs and moved to rise. "Can I go now?"

"No. That was the only item on the agenda, but this is an opportunity for anyone to raise any issues that they may have." Fergal dropped the roll of paper on the table. "Do you want to raise an issue?"

"Can we discuss the land purchase?"

Fergal and Randolph both winced. Three months ago, Destiny had sold its land to the railroad for a ten thousand dollar stake in the railroad business. But before Destiny saw the money, the railroad had busted, reformed, and busted again. The failure to receive the money and the subsequent lack of improvements to the town was an open wound guaranteed to generate an argument whenever two people in Destiny met.

"Nope," Fergal muttered. "That money's long gone."

"Then I got nothing to say." Adam stood.

Randolph coughed and lifted a hand. "Adam might not, but I have."

Adam muttered to himself and sat.

"Go on," Fergal said.

Randolph cleared his throat and stood. "The new railroad is operating again and some say it'll reach Denver by next summer. But now that we're the nearest town to the advancing track, the railroad workers come here for entertainment in Warty Bill's and Mrs. Simpson's parlor, and they're all mighty keen on causing trouble. And with every passing week the railroad gets closer, more of them come here, and more trouble comes with them. By the time the railroad's here, life in Destiny will be one long gunfight."

"And?" Adam asked.

"And I'm looking for suggestions on what to do."

"Shoot 'em." Adam glanced at Miss Dempsey, but received only a cold stare back.

"I was looking for a solution that didn't involve stopping gunfights with more gunfights."

"Then I'm plum out of ideas. Can I go now?"

"You can't," Fergal snapped, then turned to Randolph. "You're facing the problem every day. What's your solution?"

"For a start I need a jail."

"You've almost finished your cell."

"Yeah, one cell after three months of building. With all the gunslingers I need to lock up, it'll take me years to build sufficient cells. And without a deterrent in the mean time, I got nothing to threaten them with, so they'll continue to cause trouble."

Fergal shook his head. "We can't afford a proper jail."

"Won't be a town left if we don't."

"But we—"

Adam coughed. "Can't you two argue about this without me? I made my suggestion and that's all you're getting."

"Town meeting ain't finished," Randolph snapped. "We need a jail. It's the only option. And I'd welcome suggestions as to how we raise the money."

Fergal shook his head, then joined Randolph in staring at Adam.

"I'm plum out of ideas," Adam said.

From the front row, Miss Dempsey coughed.

"As you *men* aren't offering any viable solutions," she said. "I have an alternate suggestion."

"Oh no," Adam muttered. "I wouldn't have come if I knew this would take so long."

"Go on," Fergal said, holding his arms wide. "I'm always open to new ideas."

"I know," Randolph whispered. "That's what got us into this mess."

She stood. "I came to Destiny because I believed that decent families would flock here. And I intended to teach their children in this school and so help to create a decent town. But I was wrong. No families are here and I have no children to teach."

"If we build a jail and I remove the gunslingers," Randolph said, "decent folk will come here."

"I don't agree, Sheriff McDougal. We must address a more fundamental problem." She edged her half-glasses down her nose and peered at Randolph over the top of them. "Why do gunslingers cause trouble in the first place?"

"Because they're no-good varmints."

"Wrong. They cause trouble because nobody has taught them the proper way to behave. An educated man is a civilized man. An uneducated man is a savage."

Randolph shrugged. "Got no way of arguing with that. But I ain't sure what you're suggesting."

"I came to Destiny to teach. So I will. My suggestion is that instead of you building a jail so you can throw the gunslingers in it, send them to this school instead and I'll educate them."

Randolph snorted. "So you'll teach them to fight better and shoot better?"

"No, I'll teach them about art, about science, about the beauty of language."

"That's ridiculous. The varmints who roar through Destiny looking to shoot up the town only understand guns and fists and whiskey."

"Precisely my point, Sheriff McDougal."

"Pardon?"

"That *is* all they understand. But once they're educated, they'll understand much, much more."

Randolph folded his arms. "I ain't agreeing to that."

Beside him, Fergal folded his arms too. "And neither am I."

She looked at each man in turn, shaking her head.

"It's irrelevant whether you agree or disagree. We're a democratic town and the majority decides town policy. As this is an official town meeting, we should vote on my motion."

"Womenfolk don't get a vote."

"I'm well aware of that, but neither do elected officials, which means you." She pointed at Randolph, then roved her finger to point at Fergal. "And neither does the mayor, who merely enforces the will of the people."

With his eyebrows raised, Randolph glanced at Fergal, but Fergal returned a shrug. Randolph turned back to her.

"That can't be right. We must get a vote."

She pushed her half-glasses up her nose. The smallest of smiles creased her mouth.

"That's the joy of education, Sheriff McDougal. You learn things. In this case, about the protocol of town politics."

"But that means the only person with a vote is Adam."

"It does." A full smile emerged. "And we should put my suggestion to that vote. All those in favor of my motion say, 'aye'."

Adam glanced around the school.

"I have to decide?" he said, tapping his chest.

"Yes." Miss Dempsey fluttered her eyelids.

"I don't know. It sounds like a ludicrous idea."

"It is," Fergal grunted.

Adam glared at Fergal. "So you hate this idea, then?"

"Yup."

Adam clenched a fist and slammed it into his other hand.

"Then I vote for it." Adam glanced at Miss Dempsey as she peered at him over the top of her half-glasses. He rubbed his chin, then smiled. "I mean, aye."

She gazed across the rows of empty seats until she reached Fergal.

"Mayor O'Brien, are you sufficiently aware of political protocol to know what you must say now?"

Fergal sighed and patted the roll of paper on the table.

"Miss Dempsey's motion carried unanimously," he murmured.

Adam stood. "And if that concludes the inaugural town meeting, I'm leaving. Don't expect to see me again."

Miss Dempsey stood and looked at Randolph and Fergal in turn.

"And you'd better leave too," she said. "I have to prepare the school for my new pupils."

With brisk shooing motions, she bustled Randolph and Fergal outside.

Out on the boardwalk, Randolph slammed his hands on his hips and stared back into the school, watching Miss Dempsey edge the chairs apart to create a central aisle.

"That was the most ridiculous idea I've heard in a while," he said.

Fergal glanced to the side to follow Randolph's

gaze. He watched Miss Dempsey drag the front table forward a foot, then chuckled.

"Have you asked Miss Dempsey to dinner, or perhaps a ride in the country yet?"

Randolph swung round to stare into the road.

"Of course not. Since she came here, we've done nothing but argue."

"I know. As I said, have you asked her to dinner yet?"

Randolph lowered his head and strode into the road, leaving Fergal chuckling to himself as he pinned the election notice to the school wall.

Chapter Two

"What is it?" Gene Thompson asked.

"This, my fine new friend," Kent Sullivan said, puffing his chest and tucking his thumbs into his waistcoat, "is the Declaration of Independence—one of our most revered documents."

As one, Gene and the small group of patrons leaned forward and peered into the glass cabinet. Inside, a parchment rested on a purple cushion. Bold writing coated the parchment.

Gene tapped the glass. "And it's the genuine article?"

"It sure is." Kent's booming voice echoed under the awning at the side of his wagon. "And I'm honored to bring this priceless treasure to Salt Creek for your perusal."

Gene leaned back from the cabinet and frowned.

"I thought it'd be bigger."

"Its physical dimensions aren't important. But the huge impact it has had on the founding of our great nation is." Kent took a deep breath and stared aloft, his eyes glazing as his voice took on a lecturing tone. "Who amongst us can forget those memorable words? 'We, the people—' "

Gene's ten-year-old son, Danny, snorted and lifted a hand.

"Those ain't the opening words, Mister Show-man," he whined. "The Declaration of Independence says—"

"I think we can now all see the point of my educational exhibition of our country's proud heritage. It enables me to destroy fallacies, and I see I have a prime opportunity here this afternoon." Kent waggled a finger, encouraging Danny to slip to the front. He leaned his hands on his knees and favored the boy with a wide smile, then stood tall and tapped the glass. "Read this and you'll find that I'm correct."

Danny scrunched his eyes and mouthed as he read the words on the parchment, then leaned back and folded his arms.

"Those are the opening words of the Constitution. I've taught myself all about the Declaration of Independence. I know what the opening words are—and they ain't them!"

"I worry about our children's education when they're ignorant of our history." Kent waggled his eyebrows, receiving a round of encouraging laughter from the patrons, then pointed at the proud signature at the bottom of the parchment. "But no matter. Everyone

can learn from the great words uttered by our beloved
president John Adams."

"But Thomas Jefferson wrote the Declaration of Independence."

Kent blinked hard. He glanced over Danny's shoulder at Morgana Sullivan, his sister, who winced and
glanced away, shaking her head. He held a hand to
the side.

"Moving on. My next exhibit, the pride of my exhibition, is a special coonskin hat."

"Ouch," Danny squeaked.

Everyone turned. Danny was rubbing his ear and
glaring over his shoulder at Morgana who was staring
intently at the wall of the wagon.

Kent beckoned the patrons to draw closer and ex-
amine the moth-eaten hat in the next cabinet. He stared
at Gene, avoiding looking at Danny, who had stopped
rubbing his ear and was reading the notes Kent had
provided to this exhibit, his nose wrinkled with con-
tempt.

Gene gathered Danny to stand before him and they
shared a whispered conversation. Gene nodded.

"This hat is finer than that Declaration of Independence," Gene said, frowning. "But it ain't as fine as
the coonskin hat in Clementine."

"But this isn't just any coonskin hat. Davy Crockett
himself wore this hat on that immortal day when he
defended the Alamo against—"

"Yeah, yeah, I know, but so was the one in Clementine." Gene folded his arms. "And that coonskin
hat is a whole lot finer than this one."

As everyone shuffled on, muttering to each other, Kent sighed and tipped back his hat, then pointed to the next exhibit.

"I reckon you'll like this item of Alamo memorabilia." Kent forced a smile. "This is Jim Bowie's first knife."

Danny tugged Gene's sleeve and dragged him down to whisper in his ear.

Gene nodded. He stood and glared at Kent.

"How do we know this is his first knife?"

"Because Jim carved his name in the hilt."

Danny tugged on his father's jacket. They whispered again. Then Gene straightened.

"If Jim Bowie carved his name on this knife, he must have had another knife to do the carving, and that one would have been his first." Gene gazed across the other patrons. "So where's that knife?"

Kent glared at Danny, then at Gene.

"He carved his name using a borrowed knife. This is the first knife that he owned."

Danny and Gene lowered their heads a moment.

With this victory, Kent couldn't stop a huge smile breaking out. But the smile eroded as Gene's and Danny's eyes opened wide in unison and they pointed into the cabinet, their fingers shaking with righteous indignation.

"That ain't right," Gene sputtered.

"Yeah," Danny whined. "That ain't right."

Kent glanced into the cabinet, following the direction of their fevered pointing. He winced.

"It is. Unfortunately, Jim carved his name when he

was young and still thought that his name was spelt
B-O-W-Y."

"But—"

Kent lifted a finger to his lips. "And now I'll leave
you to browse at your leisure."

As Gene and Danny debated the dubious merits of
the latest exhibit, Kent backed from the disgruntled
patrons, shaking his head.

He slipped through the cloth doorway of his awning, sauntered outside, and sat at a table beside the
entrance. He had previously folded a note over his
plaque, which promoted a second showing this evening of his authentic historical memorabilia exhibition,
but with a glare down Salt Creek's deserted main road,
he removed the note and dropped it on the table.

With a firm finger, he rummaged through the mea-
ger assortment of coins that Salt Creek had provided.

Morgana edged outside.

Kent looked up. "They enjoying themselves in
there?"

"Nope. That irritating kid is now casting doubt on
the last bunch of apples picked from the tree George
Washington chopped down. He says they should be
cherries."

"Morgana, I cannot tell a lie—Salt Creek is an un-
trusting town."

Morgana glanced at the note that Kent had removed.
"We moving on?"

"Yup. Reckon as we should stop wasting our time
here and head to Destiny. Apparently, it's the finest

frontier town in the West. We ought to find some interest in the exhibition there."

Morgana smiled. "Can I sell them the tonic before we go?"

Kent lifted the door flap. Inside, the patrons had stopped milling around the exhibits and were heading for the doorway, shaking their heads. He matched their headshaking.

"You won't sell your tonic to these people. They're the most skeptical bunch I've ever met."

"But I've made a fresh batch and we should reach Destiny by nightfall. I reckon we can wait for another ten minutes while I sell some tonic."

Kent nodded, and with a short skip, Morgana grabbed a crate from under the table and set it before the door. She opened it and removed two bottles of her tonic. In the light from the high sun the tonic was a dull amber.

She replaced the lid and stood on the crate. As each person emerged from the awning they saw Morgana and stopped. When everyone had appeared, she held aloft one of the bottles.

"Welcome, friends," she said. "I want to tell you a story."

"Is it about the Alamo?" Gene shouted, "Because my son says the date's wrong on that—"

"No. Mine is a different story."

"Suppose I got time for some entertainment. I traveled for three hours to see this exhibition and there was precious little reward in there."

Kent glared at Gene, then slipped under the awning, leaving Morgana to try her sales routine.

"Many years ago," she said, "an ancient native tribe who lived on the banks of a river to the north of Salt Creek worshipped a god whose name is no longer known. Their god was kind and the tribe prospered. For long years beyond counting, the tribe guarded their secrets. Then something happened. Shall I tell you what happened?"

"Go on," Gene muttered. "But we'll want proof of your claim later."

"A group of pioneers settled to the south of this tribe, and within the group there was a young woman. As the farming life bored the young woman, she left her people and wandered into the hills to the north. Unfortunately . . ." Morgana glanced at Kent who had just edged outside and was sidling up to her, a deep frown etching his face. She lowered her voice. "What's wrong?"

"Terrible news," he whispered. "Someone's stolen the Declaration of Independence."

They turned and glared at their patrons, but received only icy stares.

"Well, you'll just have to write out another one." Morgana placed a hand beside her mouth. "And this time get the right wording. And get the right president to sign it."

"And what are the right words?" Kent shrugged. "And which president did sign it?"

Morgana glanced away. Her gaze picked out Danny

and the suspicious parchment shaped bump under his shirt. She lowered her head to Kent.

"Take some dimes from the tray and see that boy. He seemed to know." Morgana lifted her hands as Kent wandered towards Danny, muttering to himself. She faced her audience. "Anyway, back to my story . . ."

Chapter Three

On Monday, two days after Fergal O'Brien had resigned as mayor, Randolph McDougal slammed another rock on his third cell wall.

Despite promising to send troublemakers to the school, his opposition to Miss Dempsey's scheme had forced him to studiously avoid arresting anyone. Instead, he'd devoted himself to building and with this extra effort, the third wall was now waist high.

He'd just rolled back on his haunches to admire the latest completed row when a shadow darkened the boardwalk. He stood and sauntered to the door.

Colin Jackson, mayor of the nearby Tender Valley, was reading the election notice pinned to the wall of the sheriff's office.

"Had any candidates yet?" Jackson pointed at the election notice.

"Nope."

"Ain't surprised." Jackson licked his lips. "But you can add the first."

"Who would want to . . . you?" Randolph tipped back his hat as Jackson nodded. "Why do you want to be mayor of Destiny? Tender Valley's a much finer town."

"Because I reckon a mayor can run scoundrels out of town." Jackson looked Randolph up and down. "And I have two in mind already."

"I see no reason to let you stand. You live miles away and aren't involved with Destiny, except for hating our fine town."

"After all the double-dealing I've suffered from you and Fergal, I *do* hate this trash heap, but I'm standing." Jackson glanced over Randolph's shoulder and raised his eyebrows. "If you refuse me . . ."

Firm footfalls paced behind Randolph, but he still stared at Jackson.

"If I refuse you, what?"

Tex Porter, Jackson's hired gun, sauntered another pace and swung to a halt beside Randolph. Through cold eyes, Tex glared at Randolph, then snorted and removed his solitary glove from his right hand, one finger at a time.

"If you refuse Jackson permission," he muttered, "I'll discuss the matter with you."

Randolph gulped and backed an involuntary pace.

"Hired guns can't threaten sheriffs."

"Once Jackson is mayor, you won't be the sheriff for long. And I ain't a hired gun." Tex opened his

jacket to reveal a star. "I'm Tender Valley's new sheriff. And within a week I'll be Destiny's sheriff too."

"You're no lawman." Randolph laughed, the laugh
dying as Tex widened his eyes. "Tender Valley's
townsfolk wouldn't accept that."

With a lightning gesture, Tex ripped a cigar from
his pocket and slammed it in the corner of his mouth.

"Nobody's complained."

Tex arched an eyebrow, then with Jackson at his
side, sauntered down the boardwalk. Outside Warty
Bill's they halted to let another fight between Snide
and Bob spill out onto the road, then sauntered inside.

As the broken swinging doors creaked to a halt,
Randolph watched the fight, then glanced across the
road.

On the edge of town, Fergal had erected a shop
beside his wagon, with the wagon acting as one wall.
For the other three walls he'd scavenged wood from
the collapsed stable, then covered the edifice with canvas.

Through the open shop door Randolph couldn't see
Fergal, but he still headed across the road. He'd
reached the middle of the road when, from the corner
of his eye, he saw movement. He stopped. A wagon
was trundling down the trail, a man and woman sitting
up front. *The Sullivan's Exhibition of Authentic
Historical Memorabilia* was emblazoned across the
side of the wagon.

On the edge of town, Kent Sullivan drew the wagon
to a halt and alighted. He glared at the town sign that
proclaimed Destiny as being the finest frontier town

in the West. He shook his head and stared into Destiny, then glared back at the sign.

Randolph sauntered to him. "You lost, Mr. Sullivan?"

Kent looked up. "Might be. I'm looking for the finest frontier town in the West."

"You've found it."

With his hands on his hips, Kent stared into town.

A line of rats was scurrying under the boardwalk outside Adam's hotel. Victor Turing flew backward through Warty Bill's broken swinging doors. He lay a moment rubbing his chin, then spat on his fist and stormed back in. Three men outside Mrs. Simpson's parlor were throwing empty whiskey bottles in the air and firing at them, but their aim was so off that the bottles were in no danger.

Kent sighed. "In whose opinion?"

Randolph pointed at the sign. "Officially designated."

"Any other towns nearby?"

"New Utopia is two hours north. Tender Valley is an hour south, but many say that neither town is as fine as Destiny."

"I'll have to see that to believe it." Kent tipped his hat and jumped back on his wagon.

Morgana was staring across the road at Fergal's wagon. As Kent lifted the reins, she leaned across the seat and whispered to him. Kent followed her gaze. He nodded and lowered the reins.

"You reckon the finest frontier town is looking for some entertainment?" Kent asked Randolph.

"That's all it looks for." Randolph glanced at Kent's sign on the side of the wagon. "But take some advice. Not many in Destiny will be able to read your sign, and those that can won't know what memorabilia means."

Kent nodded and shook the reins. He trundled the wagon past Randolph and maneuvered it to a halt opposite Warty Bill's in the space where the stable used to stand before it collapsed.

Randolph resumed his stroll across the road. Outside Fergal's shop, he glanced through the doorway into the empty interior. He was about to turn back, but smoke assailed his nostrils, so he strode around the outside of the shop.

At the back, Fergal was sitting beside a small fire. A pot of cooling bean slurry confirmed what he'd been doing today.

Randolph crossed his legs and sat opposite Fergal. He relayed the news of the first candidate for mayor, but Fergal remained thin-lipped as he dripped the bean slurry through muslin into a tin tray.

When the pot was empty, Fergal shrugged.

"I've known for a week."

"Jackson's just announced his interest. How did you know he'd stand?"

Fergal poured some of the strained bean juice into a bottle.

"Because he asked me to resign."

"You idiot! Tex Porter has just threatened me."

"Tex can't threaten a sheriff."

"He reckoned I wouldn't be sheriff for long once Jackson becomes mayor. And I reckon he's mighty pleased that you won't be mayor for long too." Randolph raised his eyebrows. "So what did Jackson offer you that was worth risking both our lives for?"

"He gave me forty dollars. And with those funds I'm stocking my shop." Fergal grinned and pointed to the large bag of beans beside him. "You can buy an awful lot of beans with forty dollars."

Randolph shook his head, sighing. "Some people work all their lives to achieve the honor of standing in office. And you resigned as the mayor of Destiny for forty dollars."

"I know." Fergal filled another two bottles. "And the best bit is, Jackson didn't realize that I'd have resigned for ten dollars."

Fergal whistled a merry tune as he removed a flask of the amber recipe from his pocket. He dangled a tube into the flask, extracted some liquid, then dripped three drops into each of his decanted bottles. The bean juice in the bottles mingled with the recipe and an amber glow spread as the juice became Fergal's famous universal remedy to cure all ills.

"Despite the threat of Tex running us out of town," Randolph said, "you're looking the happiest I've seen for a while."

"Yup. Selling my universal remedy is all I ever want to do." Fergal pushed the flask back into his pocket.

Randolph glanced along the lines of empty bottles.

"When are you opening?"

"If I can make enough bottles of tonic, tomorrow."

Randolph grabbed a bottle. "And you reckon there's a market for your universal remedy here?"

"With all the fighting that goes on, I reckon doctoring will sell well."

Randolph nodded. "And have you decided how to resolve the big problem?"

"What big problem?"

"When we sold your tonic before, we left town before too many people had drunk it, got rampant gut rot, and decided to run us out of town. Now you're staying put. You can't run from trouble, and trouble will find you pretty quick."

"Even with you being a sheriff, you can still protect me."

"As sheriff I have everyone in town to protect. I can't always be around for you."

Fergal sighed. "I suppose you can't. What do you suggest?"

"That's easy." Randolph took a label and pencil. He scrawled on the label and turned it round for Fergal to read.

"Rat poison," Fergal sputtered.

"Or rat food. The universal remedy seems to work as either. Or bleach, or dye, or boot polish, or—"

"It's a universal remedy to cure all ills. I won't pervert the product by misrepresenting it."

Randolph shrugged and rolled to his feet. He sauntered away, leaving Fergal muttering to himself and tearing the label into strips.

* * *

As the sun edged close to the low hills, Miss Dempsey sat in her deserted school, reading a book.

Footfalls sounded and she looked up. Jackson was peering at her through the doorway.

"Mayor Jackson," she said.

"This ain't a social call," he muttered. "I'm just telling you that by the end of the week I'll be mayor of Destiny, and I'll instigate some changes here. You ain't getting your school for gunslingers."

"I don't know what to say." She lifted her glasses and massaged her eyes as she collected her thoughts. "Why are you so passionate about that?"

"Because it's a ludicrous idea." Jackson strode a long pace inside and shook a tight fist. "Those varmints only understand one thing."

"And if I prove that it works?"

Jackson snorted. "Unlikely."

"But—"

"I'm not here for a debate." Jackson widened his eyes, then turned on his heel and stalked to the door.

"A gentlemen should never interrupt a . . ." She sighed as Jackson slipped outside.

For long minutes she stared at the open doorway, then hung her head. She tried to read again but Jackson's rudeness had muddled her thoughts.

Footfalls sounded again and she looked up.

Randolph stood in the doorway. He cleared his throat, removed his hat, and edged forward a pace.

"Miss Dempsey," he said.

She coughed to clear her throat and regain her composure, then peered at Randolph over her half-glasses.

"Sheriff McDougal."

"I was . . . I was wondering . . ." Randolph took a deep breath, then sighed. "I was wondering if you're annoyed with me."

"And why might you think that?"

"When you first arrived in Destiny I got the feeling . . . I got the impression . . . We didn't argue then."

"Then, I believed you to be an honorable man."

"I am."

"But you didn't tell me that Mr. O'Brien was more of a tonic seller than a mayor."

Randolph lowered his head. "But I only lied to you that once. And it was a small lie."

She stared at Randolph, then gave the smallest of nods.

"Perhaps I have treated you harshly."

"Yeah. So I was . . . I was wondering . . ." Randolph slammed his hat on his head. "Why did you come to Destiny?"

"The same reason everyone heads west—to forge a new life for myself."

"And find a man and raise a family?" Randolph smiled.

"That might be part of my plans, but only when I've secured my own future."

Randolph edged from foot to foot. "And how do you secure that?"

"You know that. I wish to teach in this school." She slammed her book closed. "And while you continue to stop me teaching, I won't fulfill my dream."

"I ain't stopping you."

"Every day for the last three months you've arrested somebody for rowdy, drunken behavior. Within the hour, they escape from your useless jail and are busy being rowdy and drunken again. But two days ago you agreed that anyone you arrested would come to my school rather than go to your jail."

"That's the agreement."

She gestured at the deserted school. "So why do I not have any pupils?"

"Because I ain't arrested anyone."

She shrugged. "Perhaps you don't want to test whether my idea will work. Perhaps you're just waiting until Mr. Jackson becomes mayor and stops my plans."

"He's stopping you?"

"Perhaps if I can prove it'll work, he might not, but if you don't give me a chance, I won't be able to."

"I'm not blocking you. To be honest, I reckon the town's been quieter."

"To me, the mayhem outside is the same as any other day. Is that another lie from a man who only lied to me that once?" She opened her book and read a line, then looked back up and narrowed her eyes. "Anything more, Sheriff McDougal?"

"I was . . . I was wondering . . ." Randolph hunched his shoulders. "Nothing."

He turned and strode from the school.

She forced herself to read another line from her book, but as she'd lost track of her reading, she backtracked a page. Still, the words failed to hold her attention and she closed the book.

She stood and paced across the deserted room. With her arms folded, she stood in the doorway and watched Randolph wander into his office, then glanced at the wagon opposite Warty Bill's.

With a sigh, she paced outside and down the boardwalk, averting her gaze from Mrs. Simpson's parlor, then veered across the road.

Kent Sullivan stood and lifted his hat. "I assume that you aren't heading to Warty Bill's, Ma'am?"

"I'm not."

"So would you like to see my exhibition of authentic historical memorabilia?" Kent frowned. "Memorabilia means items that are worth remembering."

"I know what memorabilia means, Mr. Sullivan. And I'll see what you're offering."

She placed a coin in Kent's tray and wandered under the awning. She peered at the first exhibit, then looked at Kent through narrowed eyes.

"So this is the original Declaration of Independence, is it?"

"It is. I have it on loan from . . ." Kent contemplated her stern jaw. "It's a copy."

"So why claim that it's the original?"

"To educate as many people as possible you can't admit that something is a copy. But if you claim that it's the original, people come flocking." Kent glanced at the deserted exhibition and sighed.

She provided a small smile. "I fear that fabrication won't excite anyone around these parts."

"That's not my concern. Education is a calling. If only one person listens to my message, my sacrifice was worthwhile."

For long moments she stared at Kent, then nodded.

"How true that is. You only have to change one person's life for the better and your efforts are worthwhile. Thank you for bolstering my flagging confidence, Mr. Sullivan."

"Glad that I've helped *one* person." Kent watched her wander past the coonskin hat and Jim Bowie's first knife, but she stopped and peered into the cabinet containing the original manuscript of a Mark Twain story. "Or perhaps a kindred spirit."

She looked up. "Perhaps."

"It may bolster your flagging confidence more to know that I support your ideas. Education is for all."

"How do you know about my ideas?"

"I talk to people. I listen to people."

"Then you may know that I don't have much longer. If I can't prove that my school works, Mr. Jackson will close it."

"Is he the favorite to be mayor?"

"He's the only candidate."

"Perhaps another candidate, who will support your wonderful ideas, will stand and defeat him."

"That is unlikely." She provided a wan smile, then sauntered from the exhibition. She stopped in the doorway. "And for your information, I'm familiar with Mr. Twain's published writing, and I'm sure his spelling isn't that poor."

Kent winced, then followed her out to watch her walk back to the school.

Long after she'd disappeared inside, he still stared toward the school.

Chapter Four

On Tuesday, two hours into a fine summer day, Fergal O'Brien threw back the canvas covering his doorframe. He held his arms wide and drew in a deep breath, enjoying the anticipation of returning to the task that he believed to be his calling.

On the other side of the road, Randolph stood before his office. He looked up and down the road, but his gaze kept returning to the school.

Fergal beckoned him over.

"Got bad news, Randolph," he said. "Jackson ain't the only one standing for mayor. That showman, Kent Sullivan, offered his name last night. His main election promise is to support Miss Dempsey's school for gunslingers."

Randolph snorted. "That's doubled the number of people supporting it. That declaration won't win him the election."

"Perhaps he knows that." Fergal raised his eyebrows. "Miss Dempsey visited his exhibition last night. I reckon she's found a confidant. And he's found a prize worth pursuing."

Randolph shook his head. "She wouldn't like him."

"She wants to teach, but when Jackson becomes mayor, he'll close her school. Kent is her only chance." Fergal smiled. "And I'm sure she'll be grateful, whatever the result."

Randolph slammed his hands on his hips. "I ain't accepting that."

"You got no choice. Unless you can gather the courage to tell Miss Dempsey what you think of her." Fergal patted Randolph's shoulder.

Randolph sighed. He glanced at a fight that Snide and Victor were just starting up outside Warty Bill's, then shrugged and sauntered to his office. On the boardwalk, he glared at Kent's wagon.

Fergal shook his head, dismissing Randolph's problems from his mind, and busied himself with removing trays from his wagon. Rows of bottles graced the trays in neat rows. Inside the bottles, the amber tonic caught the rays of the morning sun and sparkled. Even when he carried the bottles into the darkened interior of his shop, they still trapped some of the sun's rays inside and released them with steady thrift.

Further down the road, Kent and Morgana emerged from their wagon and matched Fergal's industry as they erected their stall.

From the corner of his eye, Fergal glanced at them every time he carried a new tray undercover, but once they'd erected the stall, they just huddled and chatted. As he unloaded the last tray, Morgana sauntered to him, her long skirts swinging.

With a sweet smile on her lips, she slipped into the shop, closely followed by Fergal.

"Can I interest you in a tonic?" Fergal asked. He placed the tray on a table and gestured at his rows of bottles. Stray amber sparkles from the bottles rippled across his outstretched hand.

Morgana shrugged. "What kind of tonic?"

"It's a universal remedy to cure all ills." Fergal lifted a bottle. He cradled it in his palm, holding it upright with the index finger of his other hand. "No injury is so bad, no ailment is so painful, no condition is so embarrassing that this amber liquid cannot cure it."

Morgana took the bottle and held it to her face. Her smooth complexion glowed amber.

"How much?"

"For such a handsome young lady as yourself, a dollar."

"And for everyone else?"

Fergal shrugged. "Also one dollar."

"I might purchase a bottle, later. For now, I'm busy. I have my own stall to open."

She smiled and handed the bottle back to Fergal. With her skirts swinging, she sauntered from his shack.

Fergal leaned back against the doorframe and watched her disappear into the wagon, then emerge holding a tray. On it, two rows of bottles sparkled in the morning sun, although they lacked the brilliance of Fergal's amber tonic.

She placed the tray on her stall, then wandered back inside. This time she emerged with a banner, which she unfurled and pinned to the front of her stall.

Fergal edged ten paces into the road to read the banner. He closed his eyes a moment, then re-read it. He gulped.

Morgana Sullivan's Lazarus Tonic, the banner read. *50 cents a bottle.*

Morgana waved at Fergal, then licked her lips to subdue her smile. Victor had just polaxed Snide and she beckoned him to approach.

Fergal rocked back and forth on his heels, fighting the urge to dash to her stall and tear down her banner, but he saw Randolph dashing across the road and peering at Morgana's stall.

"Have you seen—" Randolph said, pointing.

"I know," Fergal snapped.

"And she's selling—"

"I know."

"And she's opened just down the—"

"I know!"

"And her tonic's cheaper than—"

"I know, I know, I know, *I know.*"

Randolph tipped back his hat. "This ain't looking good."

"And I know that too." Fergal pointed at Morgana's stall.

Morgana had now attracted Bob and had already enticed him to hold a bottle of her tonic.

Randolph sighed. "And this is looking worse."

"Stop being so negative and find out what she's saying. And buy a bottle."

Randolph tapped his star. "Can't do that. I don't work for you any more. I devote my time to stopping trouble from happening."

Fergal shrugged his jacket closed and stood tall.

"Then see what she's saying and buy a bottle or I'll cause plenty of trouble."

Randolph stood a moment, sighing, then sauntered to Morgana's stall, leaving Fergal to storm into his shop.

"Unfortunately, she fell into a river and nearly drowned," Morgana was saying to Bob and Victor as Randolph reached the stall. "But she grabbed hold of a passing log and dragged herself above water. She feared that the current would pull her under the grinding water. So she couldn't release the log and swim to the riverside. Without a choice, she drifted down the river, traveling ever further from her people. Then, as she prepared to meet her maker, the log washed up on the riverside. The young woman was too tired to stand, but she was lucky. Guess where she'd washed up?"

"Destiny," Randolph murmured, without thinking. "It's a mighty fine place."

"No, not Destiny. There *is* one place—and only one place—finer than Destiny, if you can believe that. The young woman had found the ancient native tribe's home. As the cold had filled her body, she was too weak to move a muscle. Death approached fast. But the tribe took her to their medicine man and he made an offering to their god—"

"I'll buy a bottle." Randolph slammed a handful of coins on the stall, grabbed a bottle, and strode away.

"My first satisfied customer of the day." Morgana beamed. "Anyway, back to my story—the medicine man gave the young woman a few drops of a mysterious amber liquid."

Outside Fergal's shop, Randolph stopped, gathering his thoughts.

"He won't like this," he murmured, glaring down the road at Morgana.

"This tonic won't just cure any ill." Morgana tapped a bottle. "It lives up to its name. This tonic is so powerful, it can even bring people back from the dead."

"I'll buy a bottle," Bob said, quickly followed by Victor.

Randolph strode into Fergal's shop, drowning out Bob's and Victor's enthusiastic comments, and held up his bottle of Morgana's Lazarus Tonic.

"What's the tonic like?" Fergal asked.

"Forget that. You got bigger problems." Randolph took a deep breath. "Her claims for her tonic are even more outlandish than yours are. She not only claims that it'll cure all ills, she claims it'll bring people back from the dead."

Fergal laughed. "A brave boast, but nobody ever gained from understating a product's virtues. I can deal with that."

"You might, but that ain't the worst of it. You know the story you told when we were selling the tonic—

about you falling into a river, nearly drowning, a medicine man saving you, then giving you the secret of the universal remedy?"

"That is no story, Randolph." Fergal waggled a finger. "That is a true tale."

"True or not. Morgana's telling the very same tale."

Fergal slammed his palm against his forehead.

"How? Why? What?" he blurted.

"And I got more bad news. You owe me fifty cents."

"In due time." Fergal stalked to the doorway and watched Morgana entice another customer. "What does this mean?"

"As a lawman, I'm done with figuring out problems like that. I stick to the simple problems like arresting outlaws."

"Then arrest her. She stole my story."

"Ain't sure if that's a crime."

"I suppose so." Fergal's shoulders slumped. "What does her tonic taste like?"

"Now I'm a lawman, I got no reason to taste foul tonics any more." Randolph held out the purchased bottle.

"But you know my stomach's fragile." Fergal patted his chest and wheezed.

For long moments Randolph glared at Fergal, then nodded.

"All right." Randolph sighed, removing the cork. "But this is the last time."

He sniffed the tonic, but detected only fruit, perhaps apples. With his brow furrowed, he edged the bottle to his mouth and let the thinnest of dribbles soak on to his tongue. He clapped his mouth open and closed.

"So?" Fergal raised his eyebrows.

Randolph shrugged and sipped the liquid, tasting only sweetness. Then, surprised at his own rashness, he upended the bottle and glugged the whole of the contents into his mouth.

"Mighty fine." Randolph wiped his mouth with the back of hand and smacked his lips. He turned the bottle round to read the label, then rubbed his stomach. "This can't be a real tonic. It's settled well."

Fergal took the bottle from Randolph and held it up to the light. He swirled the dregs, then dripped them into his mouth. With a satisfied murmur, he licked his lips.

"It *does* taste fine. Probably just apples and water." Fergal wiped a finger around the rim and licked the finger. "And something else. Ain't sure what."

"Whatever it is, I'm sure her customers won't run her out of town when they've drank this tonic."

"Yeah, but do you feel better?"

"Wasn't ill beforehand." Randolph rubbed his stomach. "But it sure beats *your* tonic."

"Mine is a genuine product. Hers ain't."

"Perhaps, but the way I see it, her tonic tastes mighty fine, its cheaper than yours is, and she's a more appealing salesperson than you are. And unless you can beat that, you'll never get any business."

Randolph tipped his hat to Fergal, then sauntered outside, leaving Fergal muttering to himself.

In the road Randolph watched Morgana sell another

bottle, then strode across the road. Twenty yards from the sheriff's office he slid to a halt.

Blaine Sherman, mayor of New Utopia, stood on the boardwalk reading the election notice.

Randolph edged back and forth, then joined Sherman.

"Which idiots want to be mayor of the trash heap that for some reason is called Destiny?" Sherman muttered, pointing at the election notice.

"It's a battle between a traveling showman, Kent Sullivan," Randolph said, "and an old friend of yours, Colin Jackson."

Sherman narrowed his eyes. "What's that varmint up to? Jackson doesn't want to run a rat-infested hole like Destiny."

Randolph shrugged. "I don't know."

Sherman glared at the notice, then glanced up and down the road. He nodded and turned to face Randolph.

"Then prepare for another candidate—me."

"Why?"

"Because I reckon Jackson's been thinking for once in his miserable existence. The railroad's coming and with boom times ahead, wise businessmen spread their investments." Sherman tucked his thumbs into his waistcoat. "I've invested much in New Utopia, but if Destiny booms as much as it might, perhaps I'd be wise to invest here too. But if doesn't boom, I'd be wise to keep my investments in New Utopia."

"So to succeed no matter what happens, you need

to have a presence in both towns." Randolph shrugged. "I wish you luck."

"I don't need luck. I'm a winner. I never lose." Sherman glanced through the doorway at the half-built jail cell. "And I've heard good things about you. From the look of that cell, you're a town builder in more ways than one."

Randolph smiled. "I'll finish that soon."

"But plenty of trouble is coming Destiny's way. One man can't keep the peace on his own." Sherman placed a hand on Randolph's shoulder. "A busy man like you needs a deputy."

"Could do with a deputy but nobody's interested."

"A man in my employ is interested in the lawman's life, and I'm prepared to release him so that he can help you."

"Much obliged." Randolph tipped his hat. "If I weren't an elected representative, you'd get my vote."

Sherman furrowed his brow. "Sheriffs get a vote in an election."

"Yeah, but Miss Dempsey said that . . . ." Randolph sighed. "And I believed her. You'll get my vote."

Sherman clicked his fingers and turned.

Randolph followed Sherman's gaze, picking out the man who had just emerged on to the boardwalk from beside Adam's hotel. Randolph winced and hung his head as the new man joined them.

Snide Patterson tipped his hat. "Howdy, Sheriff."

Sherman patted Snide's shoulder. "With this man as your deputy, you should reduce the amount of trouble in Destiny."

Randolph snorted. "Only because he was causing most of it."

Sherman patted Snide's back, then sauntered down the boardwalk and into Mrs. Simpson's parlor.

With a sad shake of his head, Randolph beckoned Snide into his office.

"I know the routine," Snide said. He thrust his hands above his head and swaggered inside.

"Ain't a need for that," Randolph shouted after him. "You're a lawman now, not a prisoner."

"Just my joke." Snide lowered his hands, but he still swaggered across the room into the half-built cell. He turned and wiped the smirk from his face. "So what do you want me to do?"

"What do you think you're capable of doing?"

"Pretty much anything—as long as it involves banging heads together."

"A lawman's job is more complicated than banging heads. What else can you do?"

"I can shoot people. I can drink a whole bottle of whiskey without taking my lips from the bottle." Snide set his hands on his hips. "Although I usually do those in the opposite order."

"Those ain't the kinds of skills I'm looking for in a deputy."

"Don't know what to say, then. Most of the time I just do what Sherman tells me to do."

Randolph smiled. "You just said the one thing I want to hear from my deputy. From now on, you just do what I tell you to do."

"All right. When do I start banging heads?"

"You don't." Randolph pointed over Snide's shoulder. "For a start, see that half-built cell?"

Snide turned. "Yup."

"See that pile of rocks?"

"Yup."

"See that heap of lime?"

"Yup."

"See that hammer and trowel?"

"Yup."

Randolph raised his eyebrows. "Can you not see where I'm going with this?"

"Nope."

Randolph sighed. "Then your first job as my deputy is to put those clues together and decide what you should do."

"Kind of like an investigation?"

"Kind of."

Snide stared at the half-built cell, then at the rock pile, then at the lime, then at the tools, then at the half-built cell again. He tipped back his hat to scratch his head.

Randolph sighed and strode to the window. He rocked back and forth on his heels.

Snide snorted. "Ah, Sheriff. You don't mean—"

"I do." Randolph turned and smiled.

Snide muttered curses as he grabbed a rock.

"Didn't think a deputy's work involved this. Thought it was all banging heads and arresting people."

"That can describe the job of a lawman. But the job of a deputy is just to do what the lawman says."

"Can't I have some deputies, then?"

"Nobody wants the job."

Snide lifted the rock, then lowered it.

"You remember Trap and Mortimer?"

"I'm familiar with their work."

"I can persuade them to be deputies."

"And am I right in thinking that between the three of you, you were the clever one?"

"Yup."

Randolph sighed. "Then I'll consider it."

"I'll never get to do any arresting." Snide slammed the rock on the wall. "Plenty of trouble's happening in Destiny, but what with you ignoring it, anyone would think you're avoiding arresting troublemakers."

Randolph shook his head and turned to the window. For long moments he stared outside at Kent's wagon, then edged to the window to look at the school. He nodded.

"You're right. It's time to start arresting trouble-makers again." Randolph turned to face Snide. "So you reckon that you're responsible enough to go on patrol?"

"Yup." Snide batted the dust from his hands. "I've mastered building in less than a minute, so I'm ready for the rest."

Randolph pointed at the door.

Snide hitched his gunbelt higher and strode outside, grinning wildly.

Randolph watched him stride down the boardwalk towards Warty Bill's. When Snide pushed through the swinging doors, Randolph rubbed his hands and contemplated the rock pile. He'd just grabbed the first rock and placed it on the third cell wall when Snide strode back in.

"That was quick." Randolph wiped his hands and turned as, with a firm hand, Snide pushed two men to the floor—Victor and Bob.

"I don't waste time," Snide said. "These are my first arrests."

"And what were they doing?"

"Getting arrested."

"And what were they *doing* to get arrested?"

Snide scratched his head, then shrugged.

"Don't get your meaning, Sheriff."

"I know why he arrested me," Bob muttered. "I beat him at poker three days ago, then knocked him down every time he complained."

"And I know why he arrested me," Victor whined. "I didn't run fast enough."

Randolph looked at each of Snide's first arrests in turn. He shrugged. The arrests were dubious, but the cumulative trouble both men had already caused probably warranted his action.

"Suppose if my deputy has arrested you, I'd better deal with you." Randolph stood over Bob and Victor. "You two know what the new punishment is for getting arrested?"

Victor looked at the half-built cell and grinned, but Bob nodded.

"We get a day with Miss Dempsey."

"Yup. And if that doesn't teach you to mend your ways, you get another day's schooling after that."

Randolph pointed to the door and both men rolled to their feet and headed outside.

"You want me to do some more arresting?" Snide shouted after Randolph.

Randolph glanced back at Snide. "Nope. But when I return, remind me to explain to you how I operate the law in Destiny."

"I already know that." Snide grabbed a rock and slammed it on the cell wall. "I enjoyed arresting people more."

Randolph sauntered outside. With Bob and Victor two paces ahead, he strode down the road and into the school.

Miss Dempsey looked up from her reading.

"Sheriff McDougal," she said.

"Miss Dempsey." Randolph smiled and pushed Bob and Victor forward a pace. "Here are your first pupils."

Chapter Five

Seated at the front of her classroom, Miss Dempsey watched Bob and Victor over the top of her half-glasses.

She'd taken two hours to find an activity that held their attention, but now, her pupils were drawing.

She'd started with reading and writing, but both men had a poor understanding of letters. Counting confused them even more. So before she made Bob and Victor draw the letters and numbers, she let them express themselves artistically and, from the look of it, they were.

Bob's tongue protruded as he traced his tightly gripped chalk over his board.

Victor glared at his board with a brow furrowed so deeply it was as if the production of his lines involved the hardest decisions of his life.

She stood and paced to Bob's side. She considered his drawing and frowned, then forced herself to smile.

"What have you drawn?" she asked.

"This is a gun." Bob sat back from his artistic effort.

"I did ask you to draw something that was important to you."

"It ain't that. Deputy Patterson confiscated me gun, so as I can't draw me gun any more, I reckoned I'd draw me a gun." Bob guffawed and glanced around, but Victor just glared back.

"Very droll," she said. "That was a clever play on words. Perhaps there is hope for you when you learn lettering."

Bob beamed and leaned over his drawing. With his tongue clamped between his lips, he drew the outline of a bullet-ridden deputy sheriff.

She winced and paced to Victor's desk.

Victor leered at her as he sat back from his drawing.

"And what do you think of this, Ma'am?"

"I don't know. What is . . ." She covered her mouth, but a shriek still escaped.

Victor widened his eyes. "I reckon as I have a real talent for art."

Late in the day, Fergal sauntered to Morgana's stall. He peered at the pile of coins and the occasional bill in her tray.

"You've done well," he said. "People like your product."

"They do." Morgana rattled her tray. "But only because I offer a good package. A nice bottle, a nice smile, and a nice story."

"About that story—it's a good one." Fergal edged forward a pace and leaned on her stall. "Where did you get it from?"

"It was passed down to me." Morgana sighed and spread her hands. "But what can I do for you?"

Fergal rubbed his chin as he contemplated Morgana, then shrugged.

"Apparently, your tonic tastes mighty fine."

Morgana uttered a short, high laugh. "Apparently, your tonic polishes boots. And rats like it. I reckon that something that you can feed rats and polishes boots doesn't taste nice."

"Nothing that's good for you can taste nice."

"Except my tonic does." Morgana wafted a bottle before Fergal.

"We know that it tastes nice, not that it does good. Mine is a genuine product."

"Of course it is." Morgana chuckled, then licked her lips. "And you'd like to know the secret of how I make my nice tasting tonic."

"I'm not that naïve. I want to know the price of the secret of your nice tasting tonic."

Morgana walked in a circle, tapping her chin, then faced Fergal.

"I'll think about it," she whispered, then turned her back on Fergal and busied herself with rearranging the bottles on her stall.

* * *

"How was school?" Kent Sullivan asked.

An hour after school had closed for the day, Miss Dempsey still sat at her desk. Her rumbling stomach hadn't enticed her to move. The open book before her remained unread. Behind her the sums and words that had failed to interest Bob and Victor still covered the blackboard.

Bob's drawing of a gun protruded from beneath her book, the gorier half of the sketch hidden. She'd placed Victor's drawing on the corner of her desk and turned it over.

"Thank you for asking," she said, then gulped. "But I must admit that the school doesn't work."

"But you've given it less than a day."

"That is long enough to admit I've made a mistake."

Kent shook his head. "It isn't. What did you teach them?"

"I tried the basics of language, mathematics, art, music, science. But they weren't interested."

Kent paced down the aisle. He glanced at the blackboard and shrugged.

"Something must have interested them."

She pointed at the drawing on her desk, then at the overturned board.

"Drawing enthused them. Mr. Bob drew a gun. Mr. Turing drew a . . . a lady." She shivered. "But I'm trying to forget that."

"Don't despair. Victor's drawing shows he has a spark of interest in the better things in life. He probably just got the idea from the pictures hanging in Mrs. Simpson's parlor."

Miss Dempsey narrowed her eyes. "How do you know what pictures are hanging in that place?"

Kent coughed and glanced away. "I've heard people talk. But whether you approve of the art in saloons and such places, it's still art, and the kind of art that interests people."

"I won't teach my pupils about saloon art."

"And you shouldn't. But you can start there, get an interest, then move on. The same goes for lettering." Kent grabbed the chalk and underlined the A, B and C. " 'A is for apple' won't interest grown men. But why not try, A is for ace, B is for bullet, C is for—"

"I won't do that."

Kent frowned, then circled a sum on the board.

"All right. But with numbering, don't tell them that six minus four equals two. Set them a problem." Kent crouched and held the chalk as if it were a gun. "You're facing a low-down, ugly gunslinger. You were packing a loaded Peacemaker but in a fearsome tussle, you've blasted lead four times. How many times can you roar lead at the gunslinger before you have to reload or get a slug between the eyes?"

Her mouth fell open and stayed open. She winced and closed her mouth.

"Mr. Sullivan, I'll do no such thing." With an angry wave of her arm, she knocked Victor's drawing to the floor. "Mr. Jackson mocked my experiment, calling it a school for gunslingers. I won't prove that he was right and teach them to be better gunslingers."

"I didn't say you should." Kent stood tall and

pointed the chalk at her. "Just get them interested, then move on."

She sighed. "Your words are well-intended, but I'm facing a hopeless battle, and stooping to that level won't help me."

"I wasn't intentionally stooping." Kent smiled. "But I was wondering if you'd like to discuss my ideas further, perhaps over dinner in Warty Bill's?"

She narrowed her eyes. "A lady doesn't dine alone with a gentleman."

"My sister would be there, of course."

"Perhaps another night. Now, I have to prepare tomorrow's schooling."

"Another night." Kent bowed curtly, then strode from the school.

She watched him leave, then glanced at the sum on the blackboard. She shivered and returned to not reading her book.

Chapter Six

On Wednesday morning, an hour late, Bob and Victor slunk into school. The acrid stench of smoke and whiskey filled the room as both men staggered behind their desks.

"We're ready for our schooling," Bob said and burped loudly.

Miss Dempsey gritted her teeth and tapped the book on her desk.

"This morning, for your final session with me," she announced, "I'll read to you a story that inspired me. It's one of Mr. Twain's tales of strange places filled with even stranger people. I think you'll be both entertained and amused."

She opened her book and read aloud. After a page she looked up. Both men were slumped back in their chairs and rasping liquor-induced snores.

She sighed and resumed reading, her voice lowering

as her enjoyment of the story masked the irritation her ignorant pupils had generated.

The block of sunlight through the school's only window had angled two yards to the right when she reached the end of the story. Although the snoring had stopped some time ago, she still looked up without much hope.

Both men were asleep and lying back in their chairs with their mouths wide open.

With a firm slap, she closed her book.

In unison Bob and Victor twitched and sat up.

"I've finished my story," she said. "Did you like it?"

"Yup." Victor stretched. "I enjoy being read to the most."

She nodded and turned to Bob. "And you, Mr. Bob?"

"Don't rightly know." Bob clattered his elbows on his desk and delivered a wide yawn. "I was asleep."

"I thank you for your honesty, but not for your attitude. Why did you go to sleep?"

Bob folded his arms. "Because reading is pointless."

She contemplated Bob a moment, then stood and strode to the blackboard. Her gaze fell on the sum Kent had circled last night. For long moments she stared at it, then turned back to Bob.

"But what if your name appears on a wanted poster, and because you can't read you don't know that someone is looking for you?"

"Can't see anyone wasting time looking for a useless varmint like Bob," Victor said, then chortled at his own wit.

Bob shrugged. "I'd recognize my face on the poster."

"Would you?" She picked up Victor's drawing of a lady. "If the man who draws your picture has the same artistic ability as Mr. Turing, nobody would know it was supposed to be you."

Bob laughed as she laid the board on her desk. She averted her gaze from the picture and scrawled, *Please forgive me* across the top, then held it up to Bob.

"What's that you've written?" he asked.

"You don't know because you can't read. But if you could read, it might change your life."

"You mean it's a wanted notice?" Bob raised his eyebrows.

"No." She took a deep breath. "In this case it's the address of the lady in the picture. And as you can't read, you won't find her."

Bob shrugged. "But from the way Victor's drawn her, she looks like she's got a huge head, four arms and a beard."

"And?"

"And if she looked like that, I wouldn't want to know her address." Bob folded his arms. "So, like I say, reading wouldn't help me none."

As Bob and Victor chortled, she slammed the board back on her desk.

Fergal and Randolph leaned on the only whole length of horse rail outside Mrs. Simpson's parlor, enjoying the warm sunshine.

This was a quiet part of the day. With some of the
usual troublemakers busy elsewhere, the fighting during the lunchtime entertainment in Warty Bill's hadn't
been as severe as some days, and the chaos of the
night's entertainment was still some hours away.

"We have a strange group of candidates for mayor,"
Fergal mused. "Why do you reckon they're standing?"

"To be honest, I ain't interested. Life is simple when
you're a lawman. You only worry about keeping the
bad guys in line." Randolph frowned as he watched
Snide swagger into the saloon. "And keeping your
deputy in line too."

"Perhaps, but how can you keep the bad guys in
line if you don't know who the bad guys are?"

"You reckon some of the candidates are up to no
good?"

"They're all up to no good."

"That's fightin' talk!" Snide shouted, his voice cut-
ting through from the hubbub in Warty Bill's.

Randolph winced. "But why should you care?"

"Because if you know what they're planning, you
can exploit them." Fergal glared across the road at the
bustling crowd around Morgana's stall. "And with
Morgana taking all my business I could do with exploiting someone."

Randolph glanced at Warty Bill's, where short oaths
and barked commands were ripping through the doorway. He sighed and tipped his hat to Fergal, then
strode down the boardwalk and stood in the saloon
doorway, holding on to the broken doors.

Beside the bar, Bob and Snide were squaring off to

each other with their fists raised. Randolph pushed the swinging doors back and strode across the saloon, clumping his boots with deliberate weight. He stood beside Snide.

"You finished your first day's schooling, Bob?" he asked.

Bob grinned and patted a fist into his other palm. "Yup."

Randolph turned to Snide. "And what are you doing, Deputy Patterson?"

"I'm arresting Bob," Snide said from the corner of his mouth.

"I still ain't had that word with you yet, have I?"

"Yeah, but—"

"Lawmen arrest troublemakers, but they don't use it as an excuse to settle old scores."

"Yeah, but—"

"And they don't just arrest the same man."

"Yeah, but—"

"So, if you'll stand aside, I'll deal with Bob."

"Yeah, but—"

"Snide! Stand aside." Randolph glared at Snide until he shrugged and backed a pace. He turned to Bob. "Now, why was Snide going to arrest you?"

"Because he reckoned I was about to do something."

"Which was?"

Bob glanced at his fist. He shrugged, then swung it in an uppercut to Randolph's jaw.

Randolph's feet left the floor before he crashed on

his back, spread-eagle. He lay a moment, rubbing his jaw, then looked up.

Snide stood over him and tipped back his hat.

"I did try to explain, boss." Snide grinned. "Permission to arrest Bob now."

"Nope. I'll do that." Randolph rolled to his feet and glared at Bob. "You coming quietly?"

"Sure ain't." Bob lifted his fists.

"Good." Randolph swung his fist back and advanced a long pace toward Bob.

An hour after she'd let Bob and Victor leave at the end of their failed day of schooling, Miss Dempsey held her head in her hands.

For the first time she could remember her eyes burned with the suggestion of tears. She threw her head back and blinked them away. With a shaking hand, she unhooked her half-glasses and gave them a brisk rub on her sleeve, stilling her shaking.

She heard footsteps pace into the school. She swung her glasses around her ears and looked up.

In the doorway Randolph had a disheveled Bob grasped firmly in his right hand. He threw Bob to the floor and snorted.

"A success for your school for gunslingers," he said. "I caught Bob causing trouble in Warty Bill's only an hour after his day with you."

She blinked back the mistiness that threatened to cloud her vision.

"Sarcasm doesn't become you, Sheriff McDougal."

"I ain't being sarcastic. Last gunslinger I arrested

was causing trouble within thirty minutes of him es-
caping from my jail. You're proceeding in the right
direction." Randolph glared at Bob, rolled his shoulders, then sauntered outside.

Bob stood. He batted dust from his knees, straightened his jacket, then sat at a desk at the front of the
room.

For long moments Miss Dempsey considered Bob
over the top of her half-glasses, then shook her head
and waved in a dismissive manner at the door.

"Just go," she whispered.

"But Sheriff McDougal said I'd get another day's
schooling from you."

"Why bother? The sheriff's right. Whether you get
a day, a month, or a year, it won't help you. You can
go."

"That mean I got to cause me some real trouble so
I can stay?"

She snapped back in her chair and kneaded her forehead.

"You mean you caused trouble so that . . ." She
gulped, forcing down the hope that constricted her
throat a moment. "So that you could return?"

"I sure did. Got me a fight going as soon as I got
the chance. Figured that should do it. But I reckon I
should have gone with my first idea and shot someone." Bob jumped to his feet. "Reckon I'll do that
now."

"No need," she shouted. "I've . . . I've reconsidered.
You can stay, Mr. . . . ."

Bob tipped his hat and sat. "I answer to Bob."

"No other name?"

"None that I know of. But there's a saloon girl in Clementine that calls me Big Bob."

She winced. "We'll stick with Mr. Bob. But why did you want to return?"

"Got to thinking about what you said. I can't read or write, so if ever I got my name on a wanted poster, I wouldn't know that it was mine."

"I can help you with your reading and maybe then, you won't want to perpetrate an act that would get your name on a wanted poster."

"Sounds good. But I thought some more. Reading ain't the only thing a man needs to get by. Last week I paid a dollar for some time in Mrs. Simpson's parlor. But I fell asleep and when I awoke, I had me a sore head and no money. I reckoned I had five dollars when I went in there, so if I knew numbers better I might figure out what I paid for."

Bob licked his lips and grinned.

"I don't think I'll be able to help you there. But we'll persevere with reading." She narrowed her eyes. "And before moving on to counting, we'll review the appropriate behavior for a gentleman who is in the company of a lady."

Chapter Seven

After depositing Bob in the school, Randolph sauntered to his office, but as he passed Adam Thornton's hotel, his conversation with Fergal floated back to him. He backtracked, strode into the hotel, and tipped his hat to Adam, who was sitting behind his reception desk.

"Adam," he said, "who are you supporting in the election?"

"Got a problem there. I hate Sherman. I hate Jackson. And that Kent Sullivan seems an idiot. Plus I voted earlier in the week, so I reckon that'll do me for democracy." Adam raised his eyebrows. "And you?"

"Got the same problem as you—two men I don't trust and an idiot."

Randolph and Adam shared a laugh.

Randolph turned and paced to the door. But in the

63

doorway he slammed a hand against his forehead and turned back.

"Oh, one other thing, I'm still building my jail. I've scrounged materials, but if I could raise some money, I could build it a lot faster."

"Like I said at the town meeting. I'm plum out of ideas for raising money."

Randolph edged a pace into the foyer. "But I've been thinking about those bonds that the railroad issued when they purchased Destiny's land. Fergal gave them to you for safekeeping. Do you still have them?"

"Sure. But that business busted. Those bonds ain't worth a dime."

"Perhaps. But I've heard that when businesses collapse, sometimes the investors don't lose everything. The bonds might still be worth a cent in the dollar. And as those bonds were for ten thousand dollars, I might raise a hundred dollars."

Adam raised a finger. "Correction, *we* might raise a hundred dollars."

"If I can finish the jail and lock away some gunslingers, a hotel owner will profit from extra custom by plenty more than a hundred dollars."

"I see your point." Adam sauntered into his office. He emerged, clutching an envelope, and handed it to Randolph.

Randolph tipped his hat and turned. As he sauntered through the door, he opened the envelope and riffled through the papers within.

He confirmed that the bonds provided a ten thousand dollar investment in a now defunct railroad in return for buying the land around Destiny.

Many people had been involved in this deal, but prominently displayed on every page of the bonds was Blaine Sherman's name.

Randolph nodded. He tucked the envelope in his pocket and headed for his horse.

Within a minute, he was galloping out of Destiny, heading east.

In mid afternoon, after two hours of hard riding, he heard the approaching railroad. The sound assailed his ears a good ten minutes before he saw it and a good five minutes before he smelt it.

Metal continuously crashed against metal, workers barked orders, explosions ripped out, and the ripe odor of sweat and cooking and molten metal drowned out all thoughts. The mixture clashed in a heady brew that one would think represented chaos, but which—from the evidence of the two lines of shining metal growing relentlessly onward—spoke instead of unstoppable progress.

Randolph located a supervisor and, after a conversation conducted at various levels of shouting, remounted his horse and resumed his eastward journey. This time he rode beside the railroad track and, making good time, reached Clementine in late afternoon.

Clementine was a bustling town. Riders wended paths through the carts and wagons that trundled down the main road as everyone hurried to their destinations. On every spare patch of the boardwalk people milled and chatted. From everyone Randolph detected only goodwill—none of the menace that exuded in Destiny whenever two or more people congregated. Everyone wanted to get on with their day's business, even if for many people that day's business was just standing in the road gossiping.

If Randolph were to sum up what he hoped Destiny might become, Clementine was it.

After two inquiries, and two lengthy and friendly interrogations about local news, he located the building he was looking for and strode into the offices of Sweeney, Sweeney, Sweeney and Carter, Attorneys at Law.

After an hour of sitting and tapping his foot on the floor, a receptionist beckoned Randolph to enter an ornately furnished office. Inside the office, a white-haired gentleman sat behind an imposing oak desk. Flanking him, and standing a pace back, were two younger men.

The left-hand man beckoned Randolph to a small chair before the desk.

Randolph sat, or to be more precise, squatted. A twinge of a cramp shot down his long legs as he stared up at the row of lawyers.

"I'm Sweeney," the central man said, then gestured right and left. "This is Sweeney. And this is Sweeney."

Randolph uttered a nervous laugh. "Carter not available, then?"

"He's not. What do you want?"

Randolph looked at each man in turn, hoping for a smile, but the left-hand Sweeney just pulled a watch from his waistcoat pocket, glanced at it, then returned to staring at Randolph.

"I'm here to ask about this." Randolph slipped the envelope from his pocket and threw it on the desk.

With the tip of a finger, the central Sweeney poked the folded papers out of the envelope.

The right-hand Sweeney grabbed the papers. For the barest second he glanced at them, then slammed them closed and dropped them on the desk. He leaned to the central Sweeney and whispered in his ear.

The central Sweeney's right eye twitched.

"Another one," he muttered. "What do you want to know?"

"How much are they worth?"

"Thought as much." The central Sweeney passed the papers to the left-hand Sweeney, who peered at the papers, then frowned and passed them back. They shared a whispered conversation. The central Sweeney turned to Randolph and waved the papers at him. "We ain't negotiating."

"Neither am I." The door behind him creaked open and Randolph heard footfalls pace across the room, but he held his hands wide. "That's why I'm here."

"And there's that arrogant attitude we've come to hate." The central Sweeney shrugged his jacket. "Marshal Vermain, deal with this."

A rangy, star-wearing man paced into Randolph's view. He tucked a thumb into his gunbelt and smiled with just his mouth.

"Coming here to threaten Mr. Sweeney ain't wise," Vermain muttered. "You're way out of your jurisdiction in Clementine. If you utter anything other than goodbye, I'm slamming you in jail."

"I'm not threatening Mr. Sweeney, or Mr. Sweeney—" Randolph winced as Vermain grabbed his jacket and hoisted him to his feet. He kept his hands high, but Vermain still dragged him to the back wall.

"That ain't goodbye." Vermain glared into Randolph's eyes.

"It ain't. But it's true."

Vermain slammed him against the wall, but Randolph just shook his head.

"That's enough, Marshal," the central Sweeney said. He pointed a firm finger at Randolph. "But here's a last thought for you to consider as you head back to Destiny—my offer ain't changing."

"You heard him," Vermain muttered, tightening his grip on Randolph's collar. "Take the offer or leave town."

Randolph narrowed his eyes. "What offer?"

With school over for the day, Miss Dempsey sauntered across the road to Kent's wagon.

Morgana was addressing the last of today's customers, although none were showing any inclination to explore Kent's exhibition. Still, Kent beamed on seeing Miss Dempsey and rose from behind his table.

"You look happier tonight," he said.

"I am. I had my first success with Mr. Bob. Although he was more interested in learning how to negotiate a better deal in Mrs. Simpson's parlor." She shivered. "Or how many bounty hunters might chase an outlaw when the reward was only fifty dollars. But as you told me, I had to get an interest first. And as I did, I'd like you to suggest other enticing ways I can present education to him."

"For a start I could show him around my exhibition of our country's heritage." Kent raised his eyebrows, but as she frowned, he widened his smile. "For free, of course. And I have other ideas. But first you could tell me whether tonight really is another night."

"Another night?"

"On another night we might discuss my ideas for promoting education." Kent edged forward a pace and raised his hat. "Over dinner."

She glanced over her shoulder at the deserted sheriff's office, then nodded.

"I'd like that, Mr. Sullivan."

It was dark when Randolph arrived back in Destiny. But as a light glowed in Fergal's shop, he dashed straight inside.

"You won't believe this." Randolph waved the bonds at Fergal. "These bonds are worth something."

Behind his display of tonic bottles Fergal shrugged.

"But the railroad busted. The investors lost everything."

"Most did." Randolph perched on the edge of Fergal's table. "But land backed Destiny's investment. And as that land was still valuable, the investment was too. So when the railroad changed hands, the new business—"

Fergal lifted a hand. "How much?"

"Twelve thousand." Randolph tipped back his hat and raised his eyebrows. "But Destiny's officials are holding out for more."

"We are?" Fergal shrugged. "First I've heard about it."

"Me too." Randolph waved the bonds at Fergal. "And from the expressions on those lawyers' faces, I reckon Destiny might get fifteen, perhaps even twenty thousand dollars."

Fergal grabbed the bonds and read them, then looked up, smiling.

"And we know who's holding out for more, don't we?"

"And we know why Sherman wants to gain authority in Destiny." Randolph slipped off the table edge. "He ain't getting away with this."

Fergal jumped to his feet and held the bonds before Randolph. With a steady rhythm, he tapped them against his chest.

"Don't say anything," he whispered from the corner of his mouth.

Randolph grabbed the bonds and paced to the door, shaking his head.

"I can't do that. I'm a lawman. I have principles."

"You've always had principles," Fergal shouted as Randolph reached the door. "That's why we get along. You're the conscience I never had."

Randolph stopped before the door. "So you know I can't let Sherman sell out Destiny."

"But if you talk, nobody will vote for Sherman. Then if Kent wins, you'll lose Miss Dempsey. And if

Jackson wins, Tex will want your job—and maybe your life."

"And perhaps yours too." Randolph shook his head. "I'll keep quiet. But I won't help you profit from this."

"So I'd better not ask you to help me break into Kent's wagon either." Fergal smiled. "I'm finding out how Morgana makes her nice tasting tonic."

"I ain't helping you with that." Randolph kicked open the door. "As we're friends, I'll push my principles and not arrest you, but if they catch you, I *will* do my duty."

"But with your help, they won't catch me."

"Fergal, I'm a lawman."

"Would it change your mind if I told you that Kent, Morgana and Miss Dempsey are having dinner in Warty Bill's?"

"I'm glad Miss Dempsey and Morgana are getting friendly."

"Miss Dempsey and Kent are getting friendly. Morgana's their chaperone."

Randolph winced. He opened and closed his fists, then swiveled back to face Fergal, his jaw set firm.

"How were you planning on breaking into the wagon?"

"That's more like the old Randolph." Fergal laughed and scurried past him. "Come on. I'll show you."

Randolph hurried to follow Fergal. "But I still don't like you stealing her recipe."

"I'm borrowing it. Just like she borrowed my story."

"You figured out how Morgana got that story?"

"I asked her." Fergal stopped outside Kent's wagon. "She said it was passed down to her."

"You claim that your story was passed down to you by your pa."

"I don't claim." Fergal waggled a finger at Randolph. "It was."

Randolph rubbed his chin. "Your pa was a traveling man, so I suppose Morgana could be his daughter."

"And my half-sister."

"I don't know. She doesn't look like you. She's pretty."

"Quit the insults." Fergal glanced over his shoulder, confirming that the road was still deserted, then extracted a length of wire from his pocket and fiddled with the door, opening it in a moment.

Randolph shrugged. "Sorry. But despite suspecting that she's kin, you're still planning to steal her recipe."

"Yup. Don't know how I should treat a half-sister, but if she's my kin, she'll understand." Fergal slipped into the wagon. "Keep watch."

"I don't like this," Randolph muttered. "I'm a lawman. I can't sneak around people's property."

"I'm sneaking." Fergal peered out of the door. "You're watching."

Randolph folded his arms and kept his gaze on Warty Bill's across the road. But every second that Fergal clattered about inside the wagon dragged on his nerves. He could imagine the inevitable discovery creeping closer and all the chaos that would bring. With a shake of his head, he turned and edged inside the wagon.

"How much longer?" he whispered.

"As long as it takes to find her recipe." Fergal peered into a tin box. "What is this rubbish?"

With a last glance outside, Randolph paced into the cluttered wagon. Overstuffed boxes and bulging bags filled the available space. Searching even a tenth of the contents would take all night. Still, he took the box from Fergal and peered inside.

"Civil War memorabilia." Randolph lifted a gray jacket on which someone had stitched 'General Grant'. A blue jacket had 'General Lee' stitched on the chest. "Kent must be the worst showman ever. He makes his *authentic* exhibits and he gets the details wrong."

"I reckon that makes him the best showman ever." Fergal smiled. "It takes skill to convince people the implausible is real."

"Either way, he doesn't mind pushing that plausibility. I wouldn't be surprised if the Gettysburg Address is in this box."

Fergal rummaged in a second box and extracted a parchment.

"No. It's in here." Fergal turned the parchment over. "Although he hasn't finished writing it yet."

Randolph glanced over Fergal's shoulder and laughed.

"And he can't spell Gettysburg."

Fergal placed the box on the floor. "This is hopeless. Kent keeps notes. Morgana doesn't."

Randolph edged to the door and peered outside.

"You're right," he whispered. "We'll never find

anything in here and they won't be eating dinner all night."

Fergal coughed, and Randolph turned back to see him pull a bottle from another box. The bottle was identical to one of his universal remedy bottles.

Fergal blew a layer of dust away and removed the stopper. He sniffed the contents, then cringed.

"Yup. There's that rotted polecat smell."

"So the Sullivans ain't your half-kin. Morgana must have seen you before and stolen your act."

Fergal rubbed his chin, then returned the bottle to the box. He looked at Randolph and smiled.

"Perhaps."

Chapter Eight

"Why do you want me to sign these, Mayor O'Brien?" Miss Dempsey asked, looking up from the scrolls that Fergal had given to her.

"Candidate registration closed last night, so the electioneering can start, and for the inauguration papers, I need my signature and the signatures of two prominent Destiny citizens who are beyond reproach." Fergal rubbed his hands. The morning sunshine slipping through the school window illuminated his smile. "I stretched the definition to include Adam Thornton, but if you won't sign, I have a problem."

"There's no problem." She held the two scrolls aloft. "But why do you need two sets of papers now?"

"One is for the new mayor and the other is for the official records."

"I know, but I meant that it's inappropriate to have

duplicate signed sets of official papers around prior to electing the new mayor."

Fergal rolled up the scrolls, then smiled and lifted a finger.

"I could ask Mrs. Simpson to sign. She won't worry about such details."

Miss Dempsey blanched, then held her hand out, palm up.

Fergal gave a small bow and handed the scrolls to her.

At the bottom of each sheet she scrawled her signature, then held out the scrolls.

Fergal glanced at the signatures, smiled, then mouthed his thanks and stuffed the scrolls into his pocket.

He scurried outside, biting his lip to stop his smile widening, and glanced across the road. Morgana wasn't serving at her stall, although Victor was sauntering past and staring wistfully at her tonic sign. This time Fergal let his smile grow and hurried to a brisk walk.

But ten yards from his shop, Fergal skidded to a halt. Blaine Sherman was waiting for him.

Sherman smiled. "Can I count on your vote?"

Fergal gestured for Sherman to follow him. Inside his shop, he stood beside his display of tonic bottles and held his arms wide.

"Perhaps." Fergal lifted a tray filled with bottles from the table. The amber tonic twinkled as he carried the tray to the empty table before Sherman. "I sell my tonic bottles for one dollar apiece. If I sell one hundred bottles, I raise one hundred dollars. But if I were to sell one bottle for one hundred dollars, I'd raise the same amount."

"I ain't drank your tonic, but I've met some irate people who have. I might drink it if you paid me one hundred dollars, but not the other way around." Sherman narrowed his eyes. "I understand. If I buy a bottle for one hundred dollars, you'll vote for me."

Fergal picked up a bottle and shook it. "It'd be a start."

Sherman shook his head. "I won't do that."

"You'll have to. Destiny's townsfolk reckon you've double-crossed them before, so you'll need someone who knows how to make people do things they don't want to do."

"That person could be you, but I have a strategy." Sherman tapped a rotted beam and smiled as the ceiling and walls creaked, a flurry of dust descending. "I'm discovering what my future citizens want, so that I can provide it when I'm mayor."

Fergal rolled the bottle between the palms of his hands.

"Such a strategy can lead to disaster. If you don't deliver your promises, a town with this many guns and this many gunslingers standing behind them will take exception to unfulfilled promises."

"I'll deliver my promises." Sherman shrugged. "What choice do I have?"

"What choice indeed?" The bottle stopped rolling. "I'll answer, but it depends on whether you'll take the advice of your new campaign manager."

"And the price of your advice is one hundred dollars?" Sherman raised his eyebrows, but Fergal placed the bottle beside the tray, then grabbed another bottle and placed it beside the first bottle. "Two hundred dollars! I ain't paying you that much."

"Who said dollars? These are merely two bottles, now three, now four." Fergal smiled. "And now five and six."

One by one, Fergal lifted bottles from the tray until twenty stood in a row. In a stray beam of sunlight each bottle sparkled amber.

"You expect me to pay you two . . . twenty bottles to organize my campaign?" Sherman took a long pace and squared up to Fergal.

Fergal backed into the table, rattling bottles.

"That, and I'll answer your question—what choice do you have if you want to avoid fulfilling your election promises?"

"I ain't paying to hear that." Sherman rolled a hand into a tight fist. "Because I am fulfilling them."

"You ain't fulfilling them." Fergal pressed back to lean over the table. "And you ain't paying for my answer because you know what it is."

Sherman sneered. "And what is the answer?"

"You'll leave town when you've won the election and you have papers that state you can act officially for Destiny." Fergal shrugged his jacket, shuffling the scrolls deeper into his pocket. "And you won't return."

Sherman lifted on his heels and raised a fist.

"Talk like that ain't healthy."

Fergal cringed, but then pushed away from the table. He stood tall and met Sherman's eye.

"It ain't. But talk like that *is* profitable when it happened in the offices of Sweeney, Sweeney—"

"How did you . . . ?" Sherman threw back his fist, his eyes blazing. He blinked hard, then shrugged, the anger fading from his eyes. "Time for plain speaking. Is twenty bottles the price of your silence?"

Fergal shrugged his jacket straight. "And for my services in getting you elected."

"In that case, I'll take twenty bottles." Sherman snorted. "Just don't expect me to drink them."

"Then you have my silence and a new campaign manager." Fergal smiled and held his hands wide. "And my vote."

Adam Thornton was wiping the reception desk in the foyer of his hotel when his front door swung open. He dropped his cloth and looked up. The new arrival was Kent Sullivan, but he still forced a smile.

Kent looked around the dust-strewn foyer.

"I'd like you to support me in my quest to become mayor of Destiny." Kent sauntered to the desk and held out a badge. "And I'd like you to wear this."

Adam took the badge and peered at it.

On the badge was the slogan: "Vote for Kent Sullivan. He's a nice guy."

"That's no reason to vote for you." Adam stabbed a finger against the badge. "Politicians are greedy, conniving, double-crossing snakes."

"Which is why you should vote for me. I'm not like

other politicians. I stand for liberal values, family values, your values."

"We ain't got the same values. I may have voted for Miss Dempsey's school for gunslingers, but I don't support it. We shouldn't teach good-for-nothings," Adam waved a fist, "we should run 'em out of town. And if they won't go, we should shoot 'em. And if that don't kill 'em, we should string 'em up."

"We may completely disagree, but basically, we totally agree."

Adam backed a pace and furrowed his brow.

"Do we?"

"We both want the best for Destiny. We both want Destiny to expand with new families. We both want Destiny to be a center for trade."

Adam tipped back his hat to scratch his forehead.

"Suppose we do agree." Adam pinned the badge to his jacket. "You have my vote."

"You won't regret it." Kent beamed and shook Adam's hand. "It ain't even noon and I already have my first supporter."

With his face wreathed in a huge smile, Kent wandered outside.

Adam glanced at the badge. He shrugged and returned to wiping his reception desk.

The door creaked open and Sherman sauntered in.

Adam sneered. "You're wasting your time seeing me. I don't see why any idiot would vote for a conniving varmint like you."

Sherman paced across the foyer to stand before the

reception desk. He glanced at the badge on Adam's chest and licked his lips.

"Why would any idiot vote for me, indeed?"

"That's just the sort of abuse I expect from you, which is why I've already decided where my vote's going." Adam patted his badge. "Kent Sullivan is a nice guy. He wouldn't be rude to people."

"He wouldn't, but he doesn't know how to run a successful town. I do." Sherman reached into his pocket and extracted a badge. He held it out. "And I've already gathered ten votes today on the strength of my election slogan and it ain't even noon."

Adam took the badge and held it up to the light.

"Vote for Blaine Sherman," he read, "and vote for a prosperous future." Adam snorted and handed the badge back to Sherman. "Ain't convincing me."

Sherman tucked his thumbs into his waistcoat.

"Perhaps not, but my slogan has an alternate version." Sherman lowered his voice and leaned on the desk to place his face beside Adam's. "And it's one you should only whisper."

"What's that?" Adam whispered.

"Pledge your vote to me and I'll give you fifty dollars."

Adam snapped back from Sherman, sneering.

"You won't bribe me."

Sherman considered Adam a moment, then nodded.

"But my alternate slogan has a second line." Sherman raised his eyebrows. "When you've voted for me, I'll give you another fifty dollars."

Adam gulped. But he stood tall and folded his arms.

"Your bribes might have worked on others. But I have principles. You won't buy my vote."

"Perhaps not, but for my more discerning supporters, I'm also offering something more enticing than money."

"Nothing's more enticing than money."

Sherman sauntered around the desk and laid a friendly hand on Adam's shoulder. He looked around the decrepit foyer, lingering his gaze on a dead rat, then on the huge hole in the center of Adam's stairs.

"I have influential friends who'll visit Destiny when I'm mayor. They'll want somewhere to stay and, as this is the only hotel in town, they'll stay here. But as it's such a trash heap, I'll need you to refurbish to meet their sophisticated tastes." Sherman raised his eyebrows. "And I'll pay for the refurbishment."

Adam whistled under his breath. "Perhaps I might vote for you."

Sherman grasped the badge on Adam's chest and unhooked it. With a conspiratorial smile, he dropped it on the desk and pinned his own badge in its place.

"Glad we have an understanding."

Adam shrugged from Sherman's grasp. "I'm voting for you for the good of Destiny, not for the bribe, you understand?"

"Of course." Sherman extracted a wad of bills from his pocket and held it out. He looked away as Adam swiped it from his hand. "I'll return after the election with the second installment, and we can discuss the improvements you need."

"I'll make a list."

Sherman sauntered to the door, but stopped in the doorway. He rocked back and forth on his heels, then turned.

"One other matter. I've had an idea that will add funds to the town's coffers." Sherman sauntered back to Adam's desk and leaned on it. "Destiny had a stake in the railroad, but that collapsed when the business folded."

Adam grunted. "We're all well aware of that."

"I reckon it might be possible—no promises, mind— for my influential friends to reclaim some of the funds, perhaps two or even three cents on the dollar. With a ten thousand dollar investment, that's worth pursuing."

"Pursue away."

"But I'll need the bonds to start the process."

"Ain't got them. Sheriff McDougal had the same idea. He has them."

Sherman's eyes flared. "Randolph, I should have . . . I'll get the bonds from him, then."

Sherman stalked to the door. On the boardwalk, he beckoned into the road and Snide approached. The two men shared low words. Then Snide shook a fist, turned on his heel, and stalked towards the sheriff's office.

Adam shrugged. He picked up his cloth and swiped Kent's badge to the floor, then resumed cleaning.

The door edged open and Colin Jackson sauntered in.

Adam snorted. "I hardly ever see a politician, then within hours of the election starting, I see them all."

"But I hope you haven't promised your vote to anyone yet."

Adam shrugged his jacket straight, enjoying the extra weight in his inside pocket.

"Depends. What you offering?"

Jackson sauntered across the foyer and stood before the desk. He glanced at the badge on Adam's chest and chuckled.

"I have a good case. And it's better than the bribes that two-bit varmint Fergal O'Brien has persuaded Sherman to offer everyone."

"Fergal is helping Sherman?" Adam breathed deeply through his nostrils as Sherman nodded, but he shrugged and tapped his badge. "Despite Fergal's involvement, I've pledged myself to Sherman because of his vision of Destiny's future."

"Of course you have." Jackson slipped a badge from his pocket and held it out. "And if that's your real reason, you need to consider my vision too."

Adam took the badge and read it. On it was the slogan: "Vote for Colin Jackson or . . ."

Adam furrowed his brow, then turned the badge over. The other side was blank.

"What kind of slogan is that? Vote for you or . . ." He narrowed his eyes. "Or what?"

Jackson clicked his fingers and the door crashed open.

Tex Porter swaggered in. He sauntered across the foyer and swung to a halt before the desk. With his cold gaze set on Adam, he removed his solitary glove, one finger at a time, and flicked up the corners of his mouth with the grimmest of smiles.

"Or what?" he whispered.

Adam gulped. "That's still my question."

Tex arched an eyebrow. "It depends on how good an imagination you got."

"I ain't got an imagination."

"Then for you the slogan might be—Vote for Colin Jackson or I'll break your legs. Or maybe—Vote for Colin Jackson or I'll ram your teeth so far down your throat you'll—"

"I get the idea," Adam shrieked.

"I thought you might." Tex shrugged his jacket and slammed a cigar into the corner of his mouth. "Reckoned as that campaign slogan would catch the mood of the populace."

Jackson paced forward. "So can I count on your vote?"

Adam patted the bulge in his inside pocket. He glanced at Tex, then ripped Sherman's badge from his jacket and threw it over his shoulder. Even as it clattered to a halt, he'd already pinned on Jackson's badge.

"Reckon as you can."

"Good." Jackson turned. "That's eleven votes already and it ain't even noon."

Jackson strode outside, whistling under his breath. But out on the boardwalk, he halted.

Ten paces into the road Blaine Sherman was glaring at him.

"What you doing, Jackson?" Sherman muttered.

With deliberate slow paces, Jackson stalked sideways into the road. He looked Sherman up and down and sneered.

"Gaining support to be the mayor of Destiny."

"You don't want to be mayor." Sherman snorted. "You only want what I want. Everyone knows that Tender Valley folk are slow on the uptake. You have no vision other than to follow your betters."

"I ain't following you. I stood first."

"Only because I put the thought in your mind."

"Then that was your mistake. I've been looking for a way to permanently wipe that smug grin off your face for years." Jackson glanced to his side. "Now I have the man to do it."

From Adam's hotel Tex Porter emerged and strode into the road to stand beside Jackson. He raised an eyebrow.

"I'd heard about him." Sherman chuckled and nodded down the road. "But you'll need more than a hired gun on your side to win this election."

Jackson and Tex turned. From the doorway of the sheriff's office, Snide was pacing down the road to join Sherman.

"You mean him?" Jackson said. He shook his head, laughing.

Tex joined in the laughter, the sound deep and humorless.

"Yeah," Snide said. He halted beside Sherman and hitched his gunbelt. "I don't fear anyone."

"So, I got a hired gun. You got an idiot."

"That's Deputy Idiot . . ." Snide coughed. "Deputy Patterson to you."

Jackson looked at each man in turn. He shook his

head, a smile on his lips, then sauntered in a long arc around them.

In the middle of the road Tex appraised Snide with a firm gaze, then uttered a deep snort and followed Jackson.

Snide moved to return to the sheriff's office, but Sherman grabbed his arm and pulled him back.

"Snide," he whispered. "I reckon Tex is using force to win votes for Jackson. You have to do something."

Snide ground a fist into his other palm. "No trouble, boss. Just tell me who you want me to intimidate and I'll bang heads until you get all the votes you want."

"I don't want you to intimidate the townsfolk. I want you to intimidate Tex."

Snide blanched. He glanced at Tex's receding back.

"Intimidate Tex? You must be joking." Snide grinned, searching for a hint of amusement in Sherman's cold eyes. Finding none, he hung his head a moment. "Nobody can intimidate a man like Tex."

"If you don't, I won't make you sheriff of Destiny on Saturday."

Snide blew out his cheeks as he watched Tex follow Jackson into Warty Bill's. His eyes brightened and a real grin emerged.

"This sounds like a job for Trap and Mortimer."

"You ain't as stupid as you look." Sherman chuckled. He leaned to Snide and raised his eyebrows. "A good lawman always gets his deputies to do the hardest jobs."

Sherman patted Snide's shoulder and sauntered away.

When Sherman strode into Mrs. Simpson's parlor, Snide sighed.

"Just hope you can rustle up some more deputies for me later."

Chapter Nine

With the worry of a possible confrontation with Tex furrowing his brow, Snide leaned over the bar in Warty Bill's, searching for a way out in the whiskey that he swirled before him. But when he failed to find any comfort, he turned and leaned back against the bar.

The usual collection of rowdy railroad workers was littering up the saloon; at one table, Bob was hunched over a poker hand.

Snide grinned. He strode from the bar and stood behind Bob, tapping a foot on the floor.

Bob and Victor threw their last bets into the pot. They glared at each other. Then Bob laid down his cards to an appreciative round of whistles.

Victor snorted and threw down his cards.

"Ain't seeing how you knew I were bluffing," he muttered.

"That's," Bob said, "I *don't understand* how you knew I was bluffing."

Victor scraped back his chair and stood. "You trying to insult me?"

"No." Bob stood, raising his hands. "Good grammar is the foundation of civilization."

Victor's eyes glazed. He glanced at the other poker players, received a wave of shrugs, then sat, shaking his head.

Bob pounced on the pot and slid the coins off the table into his hat, then tinkled them into his pocket and slammed the hat on his head. He turned to find he was facing Snide. He flinched, then brushed past him.

Snide followed Bob to the bar. "How *did* you know Victor was bluffing?"

"Didn't." Bob glanced back at the table, then leaned to Snide. "But the odds were against him having three queens."

"And you figured that out by yourself, did you?"

"Yup. Counting has plenty of uses." Bob patted his pocket. "So when Miss Dempsey let me out for lunch, I earned some funds at the same time."

"And you ain't causing trouble?" Snide bunched a fist.

"You mean, and you *aren't* causing trouble?"

"What?"

"Aren't" is good grammar. *Ain't* isn't."

Snide rolled his shoulders. "Ain't it?"

Bob squared up to Snide. "It ain't!"

"That's fightin' talk!"

Snide swung his fist, but Bob ducked under the blow, and when he came up, he slugged Snide in the guts.

Snide doubled over, but as he tumbled he aimed a head butt at Bob.

Bob rocked back as Snide's forehead clipped his chin, knocking him back a pace. He righted himself against the bar and shook his head, then raised his fists.

The two men circled each other, looking for an opening. Then Snide feigned right. Bob ignored him, but when Snide feigned right again, he swung a fist at Snide's cheek.

Snide sniggered as he easily rocked back, but Bob had anticipated his move and slammed his left fist deep into Snide's side, then followed through with a flurry of blows that slammed Snide back against the bar.

Bob relented and backed up a pace.

Snide straightened and raised his fists, now more slowly than before, but Randolph was striding through the swing doors. Randolph stormed to the bar and grabbed Snide's collar, hoisting him back a pace.

"What you two fighting about now?" he muttered.

Snide shrugged from Randolph's grip. "We're fighting about whether you should say ain't or aren't."

"At least you're fighting about something different." Randolph turned to Bob. "But I'm disappointed in you. And I'm sure Miss Dempsey will be too."

"Snide was the only one looking for trouble," Bob

said. "I was trying to avoid it. And I'll stand you both a drink to show my good intentions."

Snide grinned, but Randolph grabbed his shoulder and pointed him towards the door.

"Snide, you don't get a whiskey. You get to build the cell again."

As Snide sloped to the door, muttering, Bob ordered two whiskies.

Warty Bill slopped the drinks beside Bob, and Bob slammed a pile of coins on the bar, then edged some aside.

"That was a mess of beans," Bob said, "four whiskies and a cigar, which comes to . . . One dollar fifteen cents. That's the exact money, Bill."

With his eyes wide, Warty Bill scooped up the coins.

Bob knocked back his whiskey, tipped his hat to Randolph, then sauntered from the saloon.

As Randolph sipped his whiskey, he watched Bob wander past the window. Then, feeling as bemused as Warty Bill looked, he knocked back his whiskey and sauntered to the door to watch Bob stride past Mrs. Simpson's parlor and into the school.

Randolph shook his head and headed to his office. He was still shaking his head at Bob's courteous attitude when he opened the sheriff's office door.

Snide hadn't added more rocks to the third wall of the cell, but he *was* riffling through the desk. Papers littered the desktop and floor.

"Snide," Randolph muttered. "What are you doing?"

Snide flinched, then turned and thrust a handful of papers behind his back. But as Randolph glared at him, he hurled the papers on the desk.

"Just trying to find out if correcting grammar is a crime."

Randolph sauntered to the desk and glanced at the slew of papers containing arrest warrants, wanted posters, fanciful drawings of a huge jail. He grabbed a warrant and held it before Snide.

"Can you read this?"

Snide glanced at the warrant. "Ain't had a need to learn reading."

"Thought as much. So how will you know when you've found the bonds?"

Snide gulped. "How did you know I was looking for them?"

"I'm the sheriff. It's my job to know things. And when you've proved you're a real deputy, you'll know things too."

Snide grinned. "And when might that be?"

"I ain't burning with anticipation."

"And I ain't liking your attitude." Snide waved a fist at Randolph.

"And that's the only thing we have in common."

Snide rolled up a sleeve and advanced a pace on Randolph.

"That's fightin' talk," he muttered.

Randolph lifted both hands and backed a pace, but Snide aimed a round-armed punch at Randolph's jaw.

Randolph swayed back from the blow. Snide's fist whistled by his face, the force rocking Snide to the side, but Randolph stopped him falling by grabbing his collar and hoisting him high.

Snide squirmed in Randolph's grip, then kicked at Randolph's shin, but Randolph darted his leg back and released his grip at the same time.

Snide's missed kick spun him round and landed him flat on his back with a dull thud. Snide lay a moment, then edged up, rubbing the back of his head.

"Snide," Randolph said, "you're one of the stupidest men I know. But that's about to change. You're going to school."

Snide muttered oaths, but Randolph grabbed his collar and dragged him across the office and outside. In the road, Snide bustled to his feet, then kicked and struggled, but after ten fruitless paces he slumped and let Randolph lead him to the school.

Randolph stopped in the school doorway.

Inside, Miss Dempsey was tapping a stick against the line of letters she'd written on the blackboard.

"You're right, Mr. Bob," she said. "L could be for lead between the eyes, but I prefer 'L is for *lawman.*' "

She turned to Randolph and raised her eyebrows.

"Miss Dempsey," he said, "do you have room for another pupil?"

She nodded and gestured to a desk at the front of the class.

Randolph swung Snide into the room and kicked him down the aisle.

With a muttered oath, Snide glared over his shoulder at Randolph, then threw himself behind a desk, but not the one Miss Dempsey had indicated.

Randolph stalked down the aisle, grabbed Snide's collar, and deposited him behind the correct desk.

"Why are you sending a lawman to me?" Miss Dempsey asked.

"Because he's a . . ." Randolph set his hands on his hips. "Can I talk to you, Miss Dempsey?"

"You're interrupting my lesson." She sighed. "But you may."

Randolph glanced at Snide who had slammed his heels on the desk and was rocking back and forth. Randolph batted Snide's feet to the ground.

"In private."

She raised her eyebrows, then nodded and pointed her stick at Bob.

"Mr. Bob, while I talk to Sheriff McDougal I want you to think what M might be for." She turned to Randolph. "Follow me."

She strode from the blackboard and toward the back room of the school.

Randolph stopped in the doorway and peered around. This was the first time he'd seen her quarters. And she was living in conditions that were almost as spartan as the conditions he was suffering in the sheriff's office.

A writing desk was her only furniture. For a bed she'd laid a blanket over two provisions bags. Stretched across the room was a wire. A curtain dangling from it provided privacy. Propped against the wall was a rifle.

Randolph tore his gaze from his appraisal of her quarters and faced her. He removed his hat and smiled.

"I've come to say something. I want to . . ." Randolph ruffled his hat. "I'd like to say that . . ."

She unhooked her glasses, gave them a quick polish on her sleeve, then swung them around her ears.

"Sheriff McDougal, I don't wish to be forward, but I hope this isn't another one of those embarrassing situations when you spend ages *not* telling me why you've come to see me. If you want to say something to me, just say it."

"I do want to say something. I was wrong about your school."

"Is that all?" she snapped, her eyes flaring a moment.

"Yes." Randolph took a deep breath. "I thought it was the most ridiculous idea I'd ever heard. And as I've known Fergal O'Brien for some years, that's saying something. But I was wrong."

She nodded, the slight display of anger gone from her eyes.

"What made you realize?"

"In the saloon Bob was defending good grammar, trying to avoid a fight with Snide, and he didn't let Warty Bill short change him. Those are changes in the right direction. So, I'm sorry. I was wrong."

"Sheriff McDougal, I've studied history and I believe you're the first man in the entire history of the world to admit he was wrong."

"I've been wrong plenty of times." Randolph crumpled his hat before him. "So if you can improve Bob, I was hoping you could teach Snide too. I reckon a deputy should be a better citizen than the outlaws he's trying to keep in line."

"He should. And I'll do my best."

"Obliged." Randolph tipped his hat and turned toward the school.

"Is there anything else you want to say to me?"

"I was . . . I was wondering . . ." Randolph took a deep breath and turned. He stared at her, then sighed. "Nope."

She winced as Randolph turned and strode back into the school. He stopped to bat Snide's hat on to his desk, then resumed his pacing.

In the doorway to her quarters Miss Dempsey watched Randolph leave, then strode to her desk at the front of the school, tapping her stick against her leg.

Bob coughed. "M is for Miss Dempsey."

She furrowed her brow, then remembered her previous order and beamed.

"Well done, Mr. Bob." She pointed her stick at Snide. "Deputy Patterson, if L is for lawman and M is for Miss Dempsey, what is N for?"

"If the lawman is Randolph . . ." Snide licked his lips. "But I don't reckon you want to hear what combining our sheriff and you will get."

"As long as it begins with an N, I'd like to hear it, but you must accept my suggestion if I believe it to be a better one."

Snide nodded. "And what's an N?"

She sighed. "Perhaps we should go back to the beginning. Please start us, Mr. Bob."

"A is for ace," Bob said, jumping to his feet. "B is for—"

"What are we doing?" Snide muttered.

Bob held his chin aloft. "We're doing our A, B, Cs."

"Like I said, what are we doing?"

"We're learning the basics of reading."

"Don't see much need for reading for what I do."

Miss Dempsey ordered Bob to sit, then folded her arms and faced Snide.

"And what do you do?" she asked.

Snide flexed his fists, then mimed crashing two objects together.

"I bang heads."

"Is that all you aspire to do?"

"Yup. I enjoy my work."

"And that was all Mr. Bob thought he could aspire to earlier this week, isn't that so?" She glanced at Bob.

Bob nodded. "Sure was. But I reckon otherwise now."

"And why do you think that is so, Deputy Patterson?"

Snide chuckled. "Because he ain't as good at banging heads as I am, so he had to do something else."

As Bob snorted, she nodded. "You may be right. But what if you meet someone who's better at banging heads than you are, and he wishes to bang your head?"

Snide rubbed his chin, then mimed aiming a gun.

"I shoot him, unless he's a mean shot, then I do some thinking." Snide furrowed his brow and scratched his chin. "So I either wait until he ain't looking and ambush him, or I bang someone's else's head."

She winced. "I meant, what happens if you meet someone who's intent on killing you and he's more skillful with a gun than you are?" She leaned over her desk and lowered her voice. "Such as Mr. Porter."

Snide gulped. "I ain't stupid enough to take him on."

"But what if you had to? What if an election candidate wants you to cause trouble?" She smiled. "All hypothetical, mind."

"What does hypo . . . hypo . . ."

"It means 'what if.' And what if another election candidate wants Mr. Porter to confront you? What would happen then?"

"I reckon," Bob said, "that a man with that many bullets in him wouldn't bang any more heads."

Snide glared at Bob, then hung his head and nodded.

"I reckon so too," he said.

She raised her eyebrows. "I can give you another option, if you're prepared to learn."

From his hidden position in a dry wash, Mortimer peered down the trail, the afternoon sun burning his back. Recent heavy rains had gouged a gully beside the trail, and a combination of rock and scrawny bush hid him from anyone approaching from either direction.

Ten yards ahead of him, Trap was on the trail. And

he was clearly visible as he lay flat, his arms and legs splayed wide, his face pressed into the dirt.

Since Snide had given Trap and Mortimer his orders, with a promise of a job as his deputies on Saturday and an immediate twenty dollars in their pockets, they'd planned how they could intimidate Tex.

As they'd failed to devise any good ideas, they'd resorted to an old favorite and decided to ambush him. So, four hours earlier they'd assumed these positions, and now, for the first time today, a lone rider was approaching, sitting tall in the saddle.

Mortimer stared a moment, confirming that the rider was Tex Porter, then ducked below ground level. He hunkered down on a fallen sod heap and peered through the bush at the twenty yards of trail that was visible to him.

The horse they'd both used to get here had strayed a dozen yards down the trail and was nibbling grass. With lazy disinterest, it glanced at the approaching rider, then resumed its feeding.

On the edge of Mortimer's range of vision, Tex slowed to a halt and hunched forward in the saddle. For long moments he stared at Trap's body, but the only movement coming from the prone man was his jacket fluttering in the breeze. Tex glanced at the horse, then sat back and stared at Trap, but Mortimer had the impression that he was somehow looking in all directions.

With an easy rolling motion, Tex dismounted and,

one steady pace at a time, stalked toward the body. He stood over it. A solitary fly buzzed nearby.

Tex wedged the toe of his boot under Trap's chest and rolled him over.

Trap slumped on to his back, spread-eagle, his slack-mouthed face coated in dirt.

Behind the bush, Mortimer edged up on to his haunches.

Tex contemplated Trap's unbloodied shirt, then his unbloodied jacket. He removed his glove from his right hand, one finger at a time, and slipped it into his pocket.

Inch by inch Mortimer levered up his cocked gun until the barrel aimed at Tex's chest. Down the barrel he watched Tex saunter around Trap's body until his back was to him.

As Tex glanced at Trap's gun lying in its holster, Mortimer stood, unfolding his legs with steady care. With a short stab of his foot, Tex kicked Trap's right arm above his head.

Mortimer tightened his trigger finger. He took a deep breath.

Tex whirled his arm and twisted from his hip, both moves like lightning. A moment after his gun cleared leather a shot ripped out, blasting Mortimer through the chest.

Mortimer's sole shot whistled into the air as he hurtled backwards.

Even before he'd hit the bottom of the wash, Tex had turned back. With a huge swipe, he grabbed

Trap's jacket and hoisted him up. He slammed his gun barrel between Trap's eyes.

Trap's eyes flew open. His pupils darted in to focus on the gun. He gulped.

"You did a bad job playing dead there," Tex said, grinning. "I reckon I'll teach you how to be more convincing."

As sunset closed Destiny's first day of elections, Randolph sat in his office with his feet on his desk.

With Snide being schooled today, the third wall of the cell was still only chest high, and Randolph was again debating whether to deputize Snide's friends, Trap and Mortimer, to let them finish the work. But however he looked at it, he was reluctant to do something he knew he'd live to regret.

As he waited for Snide to finish the early evening patrol that he'd permitted him to perform, as a test of the effectiveness of his four hours of schooling, he whistled to himself.

A gunshot sounded outside.

Randolph yawned. This was the first tonight, but he knew it wouldn't be the last.

Then he leapt to his feet.

Usually gunfire came from either Warty Bill's or Mrs. Simpson's parlor, but the blast sounded as if it had come from the school.

Randolph's stomach lurched. With his gun drawn, he charged outside and down the boardwalk. He hurtled past Adam's hotel, Warty Bill's and Mrs. Simpson's parlor, and skidded to a halt beside the school doorway.

He listened, hearing only the usual evening noises emerging from Mrs. Simpson's parlor, then swung round the doorway and into the school, his body hunched, his Colt held out before him.

"Miss Dempsey!" he yelled. Seeing movement, he turned his hip, arcing the barrel of his gun to the side.

In the corner of the school Tex Porter knelt, cradling Mayor Jackson to his chest. A circle of blood coated Jackson's chest.

"It wasn't me," Tex said, looking up.

Randolph glanced around the otherwise deserted school. He holstered his gun and joined Tex.

"Did you see who did it?"

"Nope. But I'll sort it out." Tex laid the comatose Jackson on his back. "And get some help. If he dies, he won't be the last one to suffer."

Chapter Ten

With their jaws stern, Adam and Snide carried Jackson's prone form into Warty Bill's.

Tex stalked behind them grunting terse advice every time their steps wavered. With extreme care, they laid Jackson on what appeared to be the most solid table in the center of the saloon.

The silent saloon folk backed and formed a circle around the table. As one, they glanced at each other's "Vote for Blaine Sherman" badges, then looked at the glowering Tex. Hands rippled round the circle as everyone swapped their badges for their "Vote for Colin Jackson or . . ." badges.

Randolph paced to Jackson's side.

Jackson's face had lost none of its healthy glow, but the copious spread of blood coating his shirt suggested that the glow wouldn't last.

Randolph glanced at Snide. "Fetch Fergal."

Snide shrugged. "What good will—"

"Just get him!"

Snide glared at Randolph a moment, then scurried outside.

As Randolph didn't know how to help the mayor, he edged through the circle of onlookers and stood by the door.

Two minutes later, Snide returned with Fergal, who was beaming and clutching his medical bag under his right arm.

"Who wants my tonic?" he asked.

"Mayor Jackson." Randolph pointed into the saloon. "Somebody shot him."

"Did they?" Fergal peered around Randolph, his grin widening even more. "What a grand day this is."

"Quit gloating and help him."

Fergal glanced at the blood-coated mayor and frowned.

"Randolph, my tonic cures all ills. It doesn't remove bullets."

"I know. But you know about medical matters." Randolph sighed as he contemplated Fergal's raised eyebrows. "Well, you have a real medical bag."

Fergal leaned to Randolph and cupped a hand beside his mouth.

"But don't ask me to open it. I forgot to pack the log."

"Just do your best."

Fergal nodded and turned. "I'll try."

Randolph grabbed his arm and swung him back.

"Failing that, do your least worst."

Fergal patted Randolph's shoulder. He edged through the crowd to Jackson's side and dropped the medical bag on the floor. As Fergal hadn't packed the log that usually gave the bag an authentic bulky appearance, it landed with a hollow thud.

"So," he said, holding his arms wide, "what's the problem here?"

"Someone shot him," Tex muttered. "And I deduced that without even being a doctor."

"Neither am I, but . . ." With an outstretched finger, Fergal levered Jackson's jacket aside and stared at the bloodied shirt, a portion of which had already dried in a crusty circle. He curled back his upper lip and let the jacket fall back. "But the blood flow seems to have stopped, so perhaps the bullet—"

"The bullet went in him and out the other side."

Fergal gulped. "With that much damage, I can't do much."

Tex grabbed Fergal's collar and dragged him up close.

"I've seen your shop sign. No injury is so bad, no ailment is so painful, no condition is so embarrassing that your tonic cannot cure. Well, this injury is bad and it's painful. And it'll be embarrassing for you if you don't cure it." Tex flexed his gloved hand. "If you understand my meaning."

"I do." Fergal took a deep breath. "But to help him recover from a bullet wound that bad, you'll need more than my tonic can provide."

Tex glared deep into Fergal's eyes, but as Fergal shook, he nodded.

"Like a tonic that's so strong it can bring people back from the dead?"

Fergal laughed, the sound high and forced. "Yeah. He needs that sort of miracle."

Tex threw Fergal back and glared around the saloon. "Fetch me Morgana Sullivan!" he roared.

Ten people dashed for the door. Snide reached it first and hurtled out into the road.

One hesitant step at a time, Fergal backed from Tex until he stood beside Randolph. With a vigorous rub of his hands, he regained some of his composure.

"What you looking so pleased about?" Randolph muttered.

"I know you don't like me gloating over other people's misfortune, but within minutes, Mayor Jackson will be dead. And Morgana Sullivan will show everyone that her tonic is a sham."

"If Snide can find her. I haven't seen her in town all day."

"She's back, but if we're really lucky, Tex will run her and Kent out of town." Fergal chuckled. "Provided they're still capable of running after what he'll do to them."

"You're right. I don't like you gloating."

Randolph sauntered back to the table and faced up to Tex.

"What you want?" Tex muttered.

Randolph set his feet wide. "Just to let you know that everybody is doing their best to help your boss. But we both know he'll die, and I don't want you blaming anybody."

"I told you. I'll find the man who shot him." Tex clenched his gloved hand into a tight fist.

"You won't. This is my town and I'll investigate."

"It may be your town today. But Jackson *will* recover and after Saturday, I'll sort out trouble my way." Tex raised an eyebrow.

Randolph squared up to Tex. "I'm just worried about tonight. You ain't finding the culprit, and you ain't threatening the people who are trying to save Jackson."

Tex glared back at Randolph, his shoulders slumping a mite.

"Yeah."

"Then you and I don't have a problem." Randolph turned.

"But that was my decision."

Randolph stood a moment, then joined Fergal.

Fergal was biting his bottom lip and failing to suppress his wide grin as he swayed from side to side, checking the doorway every few seconds.

Randolph sneered and folded his arms.

Presently, Snide shuffled into the doorway. In his wake Morgana edged into the saloon, an armful of tonic bottles pressed firmly against her chest. Kent shuffled along behind her. Morgana took a deep breath, then strode across the saloon to the table.

She looked Jackson up and down, her gaze catching on the blood coating his shirt. She winced and turned to Tex.

"What do you expect me to do?" she asked.

"You claim that your tonic is so powerful it can

even bring people back from the dead." Tex raised an eyebrow. "I'd like to see it do that."

"That claim might have been . . ." Morgana glanced at Kent, who pointed through the door and mouthed something to her.

Randolph couldn't tell what Kent said, but his intent gaze suggested that when trouble loomed, he and Morgana could be as proficient at leaving town at a gallop as he and Fergal were.

She nodded and glanced at Fergal.

"You made the promise," Fergal whispered, shaping the words with exaggerated mouth movements. "You can—"

Randolph crunched his elbow into Fergal's ribs.

"I told you to quit gloating," he murmured.

Fergal doubled over, clutching his chest. He backed a pace from Randolph's sight, then righted himself and grinned.

Morgana turned back to Tex.

"I'll do my best to help him," she said. "But he's lost so much blood, I can't promise anything."

Tex glanced through the onlookers, picked out Randolph, and nodded.

"Nobody is asking you to. Just do your best."

Morgana nodded. She knelt, slipped the bottles onto the floor, and uncorked one of them. With a last glance toward the group of onlookers, she stood and dribbled her tonic over Jackson's lips. With Jackson lying impassive, most of it oozed down his cheek and pooled on the table.

She glanced at Tex, who grabbed Jackson's jaw and

levered it open for her to empty the bottle into his open mouth. She poured half the contents. Then Jackson sputtered and coughed out the tonic in a shower. With a grunt and shake of his head, he rolled on to his side.

Morgana placed her hand on his forehead and dribbled the remainder of the tonic into his mouth.

This time, Jackson swallowed most of it and Morgana edged back.

Jackson sputtered again. His eyes opened. His fevered gaze darted around the room, but finally rested on Morgana.

"What happened?" he said, his voice hoarse and low.

"Someone shot you."

Jackson uttered a weak chuckle, but a bout of coughing ended it.

"That explains the pain in the guts." Jackson gulped. "How bad is it?"

"You've lost a lot of blood, but . . ."

"Spare me the buts." Jackson rolled on to his back. "Will I die?"

Morgana glanced at her empty bottle of tonic.

"I've given you a bottle of my Lazarus Tonic. It has great restorative powers, but if we bind your wound and you drink a bottle of this tonic every hour, I believe you'll live."

"Then what are you waiting for?" Jackson muttered, his voice gaining strength. "Bind my wound. And get me more tonic."

Morgana edged forward, but Tex lifted a hand, halting her.

"I'll take care of the wound," he said. "You provide the tonic."

Tex slipped an arm under Jackson's back and pulled him from the table. Jackson's feet clattered to the floor. He stood a moment, then slumped.

With movements gentler than Randolph had seen before, Tex bent and weaved his other arm behind Jackson's knees. Using a firm motion, he lifted Jackson. Then, with the onlookers scurrying in all directions to clear a path to the door, he carried him outside and down the boardwalk into Adam's hotel.

The saloon folk gathered around Morgana, offering congratulations and requesting to see the bottle she'd just given to Jackson. In their wake, Fergal's trampled medical bag lay on its side.

"Now there was a miracle," Randolph mused.

"My tonic can liven up someone with a bullet in them for a minute," Fergal murmured. He rescued his bag and batted it free of dust. "The problem comes in the next minute. But by then I'd be galloping out of town."

Randolph nodded, remembering a few old scrapes they had gotten themselves into.

The saloon folk demanded that Morgana sell them the other bottles of Lazarus Tonic. Her tonic sold for a dollar, then two, and the last bottles for three dollars apiece. Afterwards she took advance orders from the disappointed potential customers.

As Randolph waited for her fortunes to change, he

tapped a foot on the floor, and Fergal kneaded his brow.

Morgana and Kent were huddling and counting their profits when Tex sauntered past the window, returning from Adam's hotel. He paced into the saloon doorway.

Within seconds, all saloon conversation died.

As one, the saloon folk took a long pace from Morgana and Kent, leaving them standing alone in the center of the saloon.

In case Tex reneged on his promise, Randolph took a pace forward, but Tex tipped his hat to Morgana.

"I'm passing on Jackson's thanks. He's resting, but I reckon he'll live." Tex flashed Morgana a smile. "Be obliged if you'd give him another bottle of your tonic."

"I've sold all my . . . I'll get one ready." Morgana dashed for the door, closely followed by Kent.

Tex tipped his hat as they passed, then sauntered from the saloon.

As Kent dashed past the window, and Morgana ran to the wagon, Fergal leaned to Randolph and blew out his cheeks.

"Now that was a Lazarus Tonic indeed. How could it help a man with a bullet in him?"

"It went through him. But I'll leave you to wonder about that. I have to investigate the shooting before Tex decides for himself who's to blame."

Randolph tipped his hat to Fergal and sauntered to the door, leaving Fergal to glare at the saloon folk who were knocking back their bottles of Morgana's Lazarus Tonic and smacking their lips.

Randolph strode straight to the school and wandered inside.

In the corner where the shooting occurred, Miss Dempsey was fanning her face. Kent was at her side, shaking his head. Both were staring at the circle of blood on the floor.

"A shooting in my school, Sheriff McDougal," she whimpered. "This is terrible."

"Do you know why Jackson was here?" Randolph asked.

"I wanted to persuade him to support my school, so I asked him to come and see the progress I've made with Mr. Bob. But . . ." She sniffled.

Kent advanced a pace to stand before her.

"I hope you aren't considering Miss Dempsey as a suspect?" he muttered.

"I have to ask. But no, I don't consider her as a suspect." Randolph stared deep into Kent's eyes. "But I am considering everyone else."

With a sly grin, Kent took a step back and placed a consoling hand on Miss Dempsey's shoulder.

Randolph turned and knelt beside the dark smudge, but didn't see the large quantities of blood he expected to find.

"Did you clean here?" Randolph rolled back on his haunches to see Miss Dempsey shake her head. He scratched his forehead. "Then this ain't what I expected."

"If you don't know where to start investigating," she said, "I can offer my theory—I believe it was Deputy Patterson."

"Snide wouldn't do this."

Miss Dempsey sighed and laid a hand on her chest. "I'm glad."

"You beginning to like your new pupil?"

"No." Miss Dempsey shivered. "But I fear that I had suggested this action to him."

"You told Snide to kill Jackson?"

"No. To rekindle my pupils' thought processes, I show them how education can improve their lives. With Deputy Patterson, his greatest desire was to avoid Mr. Porter killing him, so I told him to think around the problem and deliver an original solution."

"It wasn't Snide. First, he's so stupid, he'd have left clues. Second, he's too stupid to think of killing Jackson. He'd get someone to ambush Tex. And nobody else is stupid enough to . . ." Randolph rubbed his chin and glanced at the patch of dried blood. "But I know two people that'd follow his orders who are even more stupid than Snide."

Randolph tipped his hat to Miss Dempsey, glared at Kent, then strode outside.

For the next twenty minutes, he searched Destiny.

As there were few buildings in Destiny, Randolph expected to find Trap and Mortimer quickly. But it wasn't until he was slipping around the back of Mrs. Simpson's parlor that he heard a gun being cocked behind a log pile.

Randolph halted. "Tex?"

"It ain't," a voice whined.

"That sounds like Trap." Randolph turned. A shaking gun protruded over the log pile. Behind it, only the top of Trap's hat was visible. "Put down that gun and come out."

"I ain't doing that."

"Attempting to ambush Tex and accidentally shooting Mayor Jackson is a whole mess of crimes, but if you shoot at a lawman, you'll swing."

"I didn't shoot Jackson."

Randolph shrugged, then paced to the log pile. With a long leg resting on the topmost log, he leaned on his knee and peered down at the cowering Trap.

Trap's gun hand shook. His eyes darted left and right. Then he leapt to his feet, his arms wheeling as he hurtled headlong for the alley.

Randolph dashed after Trap. After four long strides, he thrust out an arm, grabbed his collar, and hoisted him to a halt.

Trap set his feet wide and arced his gun towards Randolph, but Randolph kicked the gun away, then bundled him round and stood him straight.

"If you didn't shoot Jackson," Randolph muttered, "what about your idiot friend, Mortimer?"

Trap's voice caught and he coughed to clear his throat.

"He didn't do it either," he croaked, falling to his knees.

"Hope you can prove it. Because if you can't, I reckon Tex will need convincing." Randolph thrust his hands on his knees and glared at Trap. "But before you worry about Tex, you need to convince me."

Trap gulped. "Then it's lucky for me that I got proof."

Randolph hoisted Trap to his feet and pushed him towards the alley. Trap wheeled forward a pace, then with his shoulders hunched, edged down the alley beside Mrs. Simpson's parlor. At the boardwalk, he glanced around the corner and peered left and right, then sidled into the road.

With continuous glances in all directions, he led Randolph to his horse and both men rode out of town, heading toward Tender Valley.

Five miles out of town, a dry wash arced close to the trail, now a dark gash in the gathering gloom. Trap pulled his horse to a halt, dismounted, and pointed at a bush hanging over the edge of the wash.

Randolph dismounted and stalked to the bush, keeping Trap in his sights. From the corner of his eyes, he peered over the bush, then lowered his head a moment.

Sprawled at the bottom of the wash was Mortimer's body. The body lacked a jacket and shirt. An ugly gunshot wound had bloomed on its chest.

Randolph beckoned Trap to join him. "Tex?"

"Yup."

Randolph leaned forward. "So why didn't Tex kill you too?"

"He said that I could warn anyone who fancied taking him on. And I will. He's the meanest shot I've ever seen."

"I know. But that doesn't prove you didn't shoot Jackson. Tex could have killed Mortimer in revenge."

"He didn't. Mortimer has been here for hours."

Randolph jumped into the wash and stood over the body. He noted the caked blood.

"He has. In which case, I'll take Tex in when you've testified against him."

Trap's eyes opened wide and he staggered back a pace.

"I ain't doing that."

"You are. Tex can't go around killing people, so no matter what the cost, I'll deliver justice." With a steady motion of his index finger, Randolph beckoned Trap to clamber into the wash. "Unless you're telling me that it *was* retaliation."

"Ah, Sheriff. You saying that I either admit we shot Jackson and you'll arrest me, or testify against Tex and have him kill me?"

Randolph tipped back his hat. "It's a dilemma. And that's a fact."

Trap sighed. "Then I'll tell you the truth. We ambushed Tex."

"Why?"

"We had our reasons." Trap sniffed. "Hardest twenty dollars we ever made."

"It was." Randolph peered at Mortimer's body. "Where's his jacket and shirt?"

"Don't know."

Randolph rubbed his chin. With the toe of his boot, he turned the body over and knelt beside it. An exit wound reddened its back.

Randolph glanced at Trap. "See anything familiar about that wound?"

Trap shrugged. "Nope."

"Suppose you wouldn't." Randolph smiled. "But it's mighty familiar to me."

With Trap's help, Randolph dragged Mortimer's body from the wash and hoisted it over the back of his horse. Then they headed back to Destiny.

Darkness had descended when they rode into town. Randolph let Trap skulk into hiding again, then sauntered into Fergal's shop.

Randolph hung his head. Fergal had company: Blaine Sherman.

Sherman smiled. "How is your investigation into Mayor Jackson's shooting proceeding?"

"I ain't discussing that with a suspect."

"I'm no suspect." Sherman chuckled. "For a start, there has to be a crime."

Randolph narrowed his eyes. "What do you reckon you know?"

"Fergal and me have considered the clues, and I reckon you've reached the same conclusion as we have, albeit slower."

"You reckon the shooting was a sham?"

"Yup."

"And who organized the sham?"

"Kent and Morgana Sullivan."

Randolph nodded. "As you seem to be a step ahead of me, why?"

"We reckon Kent has promised to tell his few supporters to vote for Jackson. After his fake injury, Jackson will gather some sympathy votes. And those changes will swing the election his way. In return Morgana gets . . ." Sherman glanced at Fergal, who sneered.

"Morgana's miraculous curing of Jackson," Fergal muttered, "puts me out of business forever."

"Morgana, Kent, and Jackson get what they want, and it only took some acting and some fake blood."

Randolph paced up to Sherman and glared at him.

"You didn't figure everything out," he said. "The blood on Jackson's shirt was real. Mortimer's blood to be exact—one of your men."

Sherman winced and glanced away. "I didn't expect that."

"You didn't, but when you started double-dealing to get your hands on those bonds, somebody had to pay the price. And as always, it wasn't the person who had the most to gain."

"Mortimer knew what he was doing."

"Mortimer was so stupid, he didn't know what he was facing when he ambushed Tex. You stand to make thousands, but he died for twenty dollars." Randolph snorted. "I've had enough of this. Nobody else will die just so you can get your hands on Destiny's money."

Sherman lifted a hand. "Don't."

"I ain't listening." Randolph pointed a firm finger at Sherman, then at Fergal. "And don't push me either, Fergal. You know how far I'm prepared to go for you to make money. And when people's lives are at risk, I stop it."

Sherman slammed his hands on his hips. "This ain't about you and Fergal. I can make plenty here. If you cross me, I still have Snide and Trap. They may be idiots, but they're idiots who'll kill you."

Randolph snorted. "They don't frighten me."

"Then I'll buy you." Sherman raised his eyebrows. "I'm giving Fergal two thousand dollars for his help and silence. I'll match that for you."

"Don't try it with Randolph," Fergal murmured. "He has a conscience. If he's decided to tell everyone, you won't buy his silence."

"Then talk to him."

Fergal turned to Randolph and held his hands wide.

"Randolph, do what you feel you have to do. If there's nothing you want more than preserving your integrity, your chances with Miss Dempsey, your job, your life, go."

Randolph folded his arms. "There ain't."

"There's always something," Sherman shouted.

Randolph shook his head and headed for the door. He kicked open the door and took a long pace outside. Then he stopped.

He rocked back and forth on his heels, rubbed his chin, then turned and edged back into the doorway. As Sherman was smiling at him, he hung his head.

"There is something," he whispered.

"There always is." Sherman glanced at Fergal and licked his lips. "What's your price, Sheriff?"

Randolph looked up and smiled.

Chapter Eleven

An hour before the start of school, Miss Dempsey sat at her writing desk preparing her lessons for the day. Outside, wheels trundled, people shouted, and an incessant hammering started.

She covered her ears, but then a man barked orders in the school.

She dashed from her quarters. Overall-clad workers filled the school. She counted fifteen men, with more men scurrying in and out, before a bearded man strode up to her.

"You be Miss Dempsey?"

"Yes. But what are—"

"I'm Roger Thackery, carpenter, builder, and plenty more besides."

"And what are—"

"Got twenty men here, but if that ain't enough, I can get more."

"But what—"

"So, do you want this building shored up, or . . ." Roger turned on the spot, glancing around the school. He wrinkled his nose.

"What are all these gentlemen doing in my school?"

"Shoring up won't work." Roger tipped back his hat. "We'll just have to tear it down and start again, if that's all right with you?"

"Start what again?"

"Dale," Roger shouted. "Get everyone out. This is a demolition job."

"What are you . . ." She was talking to herself as Roger and the other workers dashed outside.

Miss Dempsey swung her shawl around her shoulders and stormed outside to stand on the boardwalk.

Six carts were blocking the road. Long planks of wood, clumps of masonry and bulging bags filled each cart, but already some men were hurling the bags to the ground and others were unloading the wood. Down the road two men were thundering large hammers against the sheriff's office.

They paused mid-swing as Randolph dashed out, buttoning his shirt, then resumed their onslaught on the wall. On the sixth blow, the office collapsed in on itself. Even while the dust was still rising, both men leapt on top of the rubble pile. One man smashed his hammer down on a long plank of wood. The other man hurled rocks into the road.

She joined Randolph.

"What is happening?" she asked.

"I got an . . ." Randolph turned to face the advancing Roger. "What *is* happening?"

"You be Sheriff McDougal?" Roger asked.

"Yup. And I want to—"

"And how many cells do you want in your new jail?"

Randolph scratched his forehead. "I reckon—"

"Dale," Roger shouted, "better make that five cells."

The man with the large hammer paused from disintegrating the rubble.

"But we only planned to build four," he shouted back.

Roger shrugged. "The customers always gets what they want."

Roger and Dale shared a knowing nod of exasperation at the fickle demands of their customers. Then Roger dashed down the road, shouting orders for the demolition of the school and Dale swung his hammer down on a large rock, pulverizing it.

Randolph and Miss Dempsey turned to watch two workers reach the school roof and rip up the slats.

"You know what's happening yet, Sheriff McDougal?" she asked.

"Looks like we're getting a new school and a new jail, that's what's happening." Randolph chuckled. "And if you don't rescue your belongings, in two minutes they'll be under a bigger rubble pile than mine are under."

She winced and scurried toward the school, only for Roger to emerge from the school with two suitcases. Another man followed him out with a crate. Even as she peered into the crate, the workers jumped from the roof and a blast from the back of the school caused the building to collapse.

A crowd gathered and stared in wide-eyed bemusement at the most activity anyone had ever seen in Destiny.

Sherman emerged from the throng and stood before the demolished sheriff's office.

"Even before you cast your votes," he announced, raising his arms. "I'm delivering a new jail and a new school to Destiny."

"Why start with those?" Snide shouted, as he joined Randolph.

Randolph glanced at Snide, but just received a shrug in return.

"I'm glad someone asked that," Sherman shouted. "Sullivan supports the school, but opposes the jail. Jackson supports the jail, but opposes the school. Only I support both. The school will help people who want to help themselves, but if they ignore that chance, they can rot in jail."

Sherman shook his hands above his head. A cheer sounded, gathering momentum as it rippled across the crowd. Several people pocketed their "Vote for Colin Jackson or . . ." badges and replaced them with Sherman's badges.

Sherman smiled and paced up to Randolph.

"Does that satisfy you?" he asked.

"Yeah." Randolph sighed. "Can't say I ain't surprised at the speed you organized this."

"When I get something done, I get something done."

"So when will they finish?"

Sherman rocked his head from side to side. "It should take two, maybe three days."

"The election is tomorrow. So you'll finish today."

"But that'll cost . . ." Sherman considered Randolph's glare. "Today it is."

Within the hour, Roger's workers had loaded the rubble from the demolished buildings on to their carts. Within another hour, they'd erected a framework for the school and the combined sheriff's office and jail. By early afternoon two solid new buildings graced Destiny's main road, somehow making the shabby surrounding buildings appear even shabbier.

The townsfolk stood in the road and stared at the new buildings, then at their own. Randolph didn't need Fergal's keen understanding of human nature to see the thought process that burrowed into them and took hold.

At sunset, the townsfolk were all wearing 'Vote for Blaine Sherman' badges.

As Randolph sauntered down the road towards his new office, he noticed movement in the alley beside Adam's hotel and stopped.

In the shadows, Tex was glaring at the cowering Victor.

Tex unhooked Victor's badge, dropped it, and ground the badge into the boardwalk. Then he pinned a new badge on Victor's jacket.

"Anything wrong?" Randolph asked.

"Nope," Tex muttered. "I'm discussing the election with a wavering voter. Ain't that so?"

Victor staggered back into the corner of the alley, spinning himself round. Then, finding that he'd escaped from Tex's clutches, he scurried down the road into Warty Bill's, and straight to the bar.

Randolph and Tex shared a long stare. Tex was the first to saunter away, smiling. Randolph watched him a moment, then sauntered into his pristine new office.

The only occupant was Snide, but he was sitting in the central cell.

"What you doing in there?" Randolph snapped.

Snide jumped to his feet. "I was seeing how solid the cells are, but I locked myself in."

Randolph chuckled. "Do you know what irony is, Snide?"

"Yeah. It's what this cell's made out of." Snide rattled the bars. "Now let me out!"

"I ain't. After you escaped so many times, I like seeing you surrounded by irony." Randolph smiled as he rubbed his chin. "And I reckon you can do a valuable job in there. You can work out how our prisoners will try to break out."

"You want me to escape?"

"Yup." Randolph turned to the door. "It'll test how much you've learnt from Miss Dempsey."

Randolph strode outside, leaving Snide muttering to himself and glaring at the bars.

Down the road Miss Dempsey was watching the workers finish the school, so he joined her. Together they watched Roger and Dale lever a glass pane into the school's first window.

"How is your investigation proceeding?" she asked.

"I'm still investigating." The second window slipped into place. "But your school should be finished in another hour or so."

"Mr. Thackery is most efficient."

Randolph nodded. "You must be grateful for that."

"I am. Mr. Sullivan has my undying gratitude."

"Kent!" Randolph slammed his hands on his hips. "What did he do?"

Roger bustled up to them.

"Do you want the school painted white?" he asked.

Miss Dempsey rubbed her chin. "I'd like—"

"Put away the white, Dale. Customer wants yellow." Roger dashed away.

She removed her glasses and gave them a quick polish on her sleeve, then turned to Randolph, her eyes cold.

"In my darkest hour, Mr. Sullivan convinced me to follow my dream." She narrowed her eyes. "But why do you hate him?"

Randolph gritted his teeth, trying to bottle his anger and stay quiet, but his guts rumbled.

"Because," he snapped, "Kent Sullivan is a no-good varmint."

She turned to face the school. "Don't speak of him that way. He's standing for mayor on principles of fairness and liberty."

"But Kent ain't even standing." Randolph edged round to stand between her and the school. "Tomorrow, just as the voting is about to start, he'll urge his supporters to vote for Jackson instead."

Roger dashed toward them.

"You want us to . . ." Roger turned away. "Dale, get that window moved. Customer says it's in the wrong place."

Miss Dempsey looked over Randolph's shoulder.

"It takes a big man to admit he can't win."

"Not if he's done a deal with Jackson."

"But why would Mr. Sullivan do that?"

"Amongst other things, I guess he was gaining support for your school. But you never know with someone as crooked as he is."

She stamped a foot. "Mr. Sullivan isn't crooked."

Randolph snorted. "Have you seen his Civil War exhibits?"

"No. They aren't on display."

"That's because he ain't finished making them yet."

Miss Dempsey bunched her jaw, her gaze boring into Randolph.

"I won't stand here and listen to you disparage Mr. Sullivan."

She swung her shawl around her shoulders and strode toward the school, then, noticing the bustling activity blocking her way, turned and paced down the boardwalk outside Warty Bill's, pointedly looking away from Randolph.

Randolph rocked back and forth on his heels, fighting an urge to hurry after her, but knowing that anything he said would make things worse. He turned.

Within seconds, his gaze picked out Kent's wagon. Unbidden, his hands clenched into tight fists.

He hitched his gunbelt higher and stormed toward Kent's wagon. Just like the last two days, Morgana wasn't tending her stall, but as Kent wasn't outside either, he ripped back the tent flap and peered inside.

"Fifty cents, please," Kent said, emerging from his wagon.

Randolph flinched, then stood straight and slipped into the exhibition, closely followed by Kent.

"I ain't viewing the exhibits. I'm considering whether any crimes are happening in here." Randolph paced to the exhibit of a coonskin hat and tapped the glass. "I've seen at least six Davy Crockett coonskin hats, and this is the least convincing of them all."

"You need to do better than that."

"I can." Randolph squared up to Kent. "You staged Jackson's sham shooting."

"You can't prove it."

"I can make Jackson show us his wound."

Kent grinned. "Morgana's Lazarus Tonic healed it."

"Even an idiot as gullible as Snide wouldn't . . ." Randolph sighed. If gullibility were a fatal illness, Destiny would be a ghost town. "I can't prove that, but you have a lot of bogus exhibits, I'll prove what you are."

"Why bother? The worst I did was ensure my sister has a trade, and organized permanency for the school when Jackson becomes mayor." Kent extracted a watch from his pocket and glanced at it. "And now I must leave. I've a dinner appointment in Warty Bill's

I.J. Parnham

with Miss Dempsey, and a gentleman never keeps a lady waiting."

"Miss Dempsey wouldn't spent an evening in Warty Bill's with you."

"She's already spent an evening in there with me while you and Fergal were looting my wagon."

Randolph gulped. "Like you said, you can't prove it."

"I can't. But I won't waste my time. I'd rather ensure that Miss Dempsey enjoys her evening."

Randolph snorted. "Miss Dempsey deserves better than you."

Kent rubbed his chin as he considered Randolph.

"Is the better person she deserves yourself?"

Randolph lowered his head a moment, then looked up and nodded. "Yup."

"Then you're way behind me." Kent licked his lips and stood before Randolph. But, finding that Randolph had nearly six inches on him, he shuffled back and tipped his hat. "I'll be seeing you."

"I'll prove what a scheming varmint you really are," Randolph shouted. "Then I'll run you out of town."

"You won't. If anyone gets run out of town, it's you. Sherman bought some popularity today, but Tex is discussing the election with the townsfolk tonight and once everyone has considered his viewpoint, Jackson will be mayor tomorrow. And that means Tex will look for you. You won't last a minute."

"Somehow, I'll expose you." Randolph pointed at Kent. "Miss Dempsey values integrity above everything, and once she knows what you are . . ."

"And what happens when she knows what you are?"

"I can answer any questions. I was just searching your wagon for evidence of fraud."

"I didn't mean that. I meant your working with Fergal to get Sherman elected."

Randolph gulped. "I'm proud of that. It got the school built."

"With bribes."

"Bribes are better than Tex's tactics." Randolph advanced a pace towards Kent and raised a bunched fist. "But sometimes even Tex's tactics are valid."

Kent glanced at the fist. "Are you threatening me?"

"Nope. But stay away from Miss Dempsey or I will threaten you."

A flash of anger flared in Kent's eyes. "You like pretending to be a lawman, don't you? You sneer at me for helping my sister sell her tonic. But you ain't a real sheriff. You're just a tonic seller's bodyguard. I bet you haven't told Miss Dempsey that."

Randolph gulped, his fist slackening as he backed a pace.

"How did you know that?"

Kent glanced away, then pushed through the door flap.

"I said," Randolph shouted, "how did you know that?"

Randolph was speaking to himself. He ground his teeth, then stormed from the exhibition. With his fists opening and closing, he watched Kent collect Miss Dempsey and escort her into Warty Bill's, then

stormed down the road to Fergal's shop. He kicked
back the door.

"Fergal," he muttered, "we need to talk."

Fergal was bent over a table, writing behind two
piles of paper. With a hurried gesture, he slid a thick
envelope under the pile of paper, then looked up.

"What's wrong?" Fergal held his arms wide.

Randolph narrowed his eyes, then patted his jacket,
feeling for the first time the emptiness in his inside
pocket.

"Are those the bonds?" He pointed at the envelope
poking out from beneath the pile of paper.

Fergal reached under the papers and pulled out the
envelope.

"I borrowed them from you. What with Snide looking for them, I thought they'd be safer with me." Fergal smiled, finally receiving a nod from Randolph.
"But you wanted to talk."

"I do. I reckon Jackson will win tomorrow and afterwards, Tex will take my job. And even if he doesn't
win, I'm losing any chance of getting close to Miss
Dempsey."

Fergal beckoned Randolph inside. "I'm trying to ensure that Jackson loses, but as for Miss Dempsey . . .
I reckon a punch to the jaw should dampen Kent's
interest in her."

Randolph ground a fist into his other palm.

"Believe me, I nearly hit him earlier. I just don't
reckon Miss Dempsey would approve of that. I'd prefer one of your solutions. Whenever you face an un-
solvable problem, you always double-cross everyone

and come out on top." Randolph shrugged. "So what would you do?"

Fergal edged a sheet of paper around the table, then smiled.

"I always concentrate on the most pressing problem, and worry about the rest later."

Randolph nodded. "And what is the most pressing problem?"

"Getting Sherman elected. After that, I trust that everything will fall into place—for both of us."

"Tex is intimidating everyone again. Sherman won't win."

"I'm writing out the ballots." Fergal smiled and patted one of the piles of paper. "And I just have to ensure that tomorrow, enough people will use them to vote for Sherman."

Randolph glanced at the topmost sheet. On it were the names of the three election candidates. Boxes rested beside each name. Randolph frowned.

"But most people in Destiny can't read. How will they know who to vote for?"

"No problem." Fergal held up a ballot from his second pile. An X was inside Sherman's box. "I've already done most of the voting for them."

Randolph laughed. He grabbed a clean ballot and marked an X in Sherman's box.

"In that case, you write out the ballots and I'll do the voting."

Fergal patted Randolph's shoulder. "And we'll worry about the rest tomorrow."

Chapter Twelve

Two hours after sunrise on the morning of the election, Randolph wandered into the new sheriff's office.

"Snide," he said. "You been in there all night?"

At the back of the cell Snide looked up from his bunk.

"I didn't have a choice, seeing as how I'm locked in. Now let me out."

"Cheer up." Randolph sauntered to the bars and looked them up and down. "You've impressed me for the first time."

"I have?" Snide pouted. "It just felt like I was sitting in a cell all night."

"You were. But you proved this cell will hold even the most determined and resourceful prisoner."

Snide rolled to his feet and puffed his chest.

"I suppose I did."

"Yup." Randolph pressed an outstretched finger

against the cell door and pushed it open. "And if I lock this cell, it'll be even more secure."

"Hey, it wasn't even locked." Snide stormed into the cell doorway. "I was pushing on that door." As he walked out of the cell, Snide kicked the door, slamming it back against the bars.

Randolph sighed. For the next minute he watched Snide hop up and down holding his foot. When the cursing diminished, he gestured to the door.

"Come on, Deputy," he said. "We got an election to manage."

Fergal had commandeered a table and placed it before Warty Bill's. On the table sat a tottering pile of clean ballots and a large metal box with a slot in the top. Behind the table the three candidates stood.

Blaine Sherman was scowling. Kent Sullivan was smiling. Colin Jackson was smiling even wider, and rubbing his ribs whenever he remembered that he was supposed to be recovering from a gunshot wound.

Tex Porter stood to the side, his gloved hand cradled on his other arm, but he was smiling.

Arced across the road were a selection of Destiny's townsfolk. All were trying to avoid catching Tex's eye, but they were wearing their "Vote for Colin Jackson or . . ." badges.

Fergal held his arms wide, displaying his bright green waistcoat.

"Friends, welcome. Today I discharge my last duty as the mayor of the finest frontier town in the West when I preside over the election of the new mayor.

And I trust that the election will be fair, and free from all bribery, corruption and intimidation."

"Why?" Victor shouted from the crowd. "Are all the candidates standing down?"

"That was uncalled for." Fergal gestured with his palms facing down, subduing the chuckles that were drifting around the crowd. "But with no further ado, I declare that the voting can start."

Kent stepped up to the table. "And with the commencement of voting, I'd like to make a speech."

"You won't," Fergal snapped. "No speeches during voting time. You had the chance beforehand."

"My speech won't come from a mayoral candidate, but from a voter." Kent slapped a hand over Fergal's mouth as Fergal opened it to complain, and raised his other hand aloft. "I'm voting for Colin Jackson. He's the only man for mayor."

As Tex's smile widened, a sympathetic cheer arose from the crowd.

"You finished?" Fergal asked, shrugging from Kent's grip.

"Nope. I'd like to . . ." Kent narrowed his eyes. "What's happening?"

Fergal, then the whole crowd, turned to watch a cart hurtle into town. The driver pulled back on the reins and leapt down even while the cart was halting. With a grim face, he dashed round the cart and leapt on to the back. Five seconds later he emerged, a limp boy draped in his arms.

"What's wrong, sir?" Fergal shouted.

"I'm Gene Thompson. This is Danny, my son, he got something . . ."

Gene sobbed and hung his head. Then, with a roll of his shoulders, he stared at the crowd.

In stony silence the crowd parted, clearing a path to Warty Bill's. Some people even removed their hats.

Gene nodded left and right as he edged through the throng. In his arms Danny lay, his mouth wide open, his slack arms and legs swaying with Gene's motion. Clammy sweat coated his brow and stuck his clothes to his bony frame.

As Gene strode into Warty Bill's, Bob peeled off and pushed through the crowd to reach Kent's wagon. Moments later he returned with Morgana in tow.

In a limp hand she clutched a tonic bottle, but her head was hung and her gait slow. Bob urged her to hurry, but she shuffled into Warty Bill's, followed closely by Kent.

The crowd surged toward the entrance to Warty Bill's, but Randolph and Snide guarded the boardwalk and shooed everybody back, although Randolph let Fergal look through the window.

With a space cleared, he joined Fergal.

Gene had placed Danny on the table on which Morgana had "cured" Jackson. Morgana and Gene shared a low conversation. Then she leaned over Danny. She laid a hand on the prone boy's forehead, then stood back, shaking her head.

"I didn't know any families lived nearby," Randolph whispered.

"Neither did I." Fergal shrugged. "But let's hope

this boy gets the chance to have Miss Dempsey teach him."

Randolph turned and stared at Fergal until Fergal looked at him.

"Did you organize this?"

"Pardon?"

"Morgana and Kent persuaded Jackson to pretend to get better and prove that her tonic works, so I reckon you've paid Gene to pretend his child is ill so that you can prove it doesn't work. Then you'll feed Danny your tonic and . . ." Randolph raised his eyebrows.

"You've hurt me with that accusation," Fergal snapped, his eyes colder than Randolph had ever seen. "You know where I draw the line."

"No, I don't. I ain't seen you draw."

"Well, this is it. I wouldn't use a child to gain an advantage."

"But what about Morgana?" Randolph leaned to Fergal. "Has she got even less principles than you have?"

"I don't know." Fergal narrowed his eyes and pointed into the saloon. "But I don't reckon she's organized this. She's gaining nothing."

Randolph followed Fergal's gaze.

Morgana was standing back from Danny. She spoke to Gene, but her voice caught and she backed away, shaking her head.

Gene sobbed, then stilled it by biting a knuckle. He leaned over the comatose Danny, his head bowed.

With her head still shaking, Morgana backed outside. On the boardwalk, she turned and, seeing the semicircle of expectant people watching outside Warty Bill's, she wiped a tear from her eye and lowered her head.

"Can you help the child?" Randolph asked.

"No," Morgana croaked. As she paced towards them, she coughed to clear her throat and wiped her damp cheeks. "Danny has a fever. He's been asleep for a day and I don't know what caused it. Gene came here, looking for some doctoring, but there's only me. And Danny needs more than a restorative tonic."

Randolph nodded, then glanced at Fergal.

"What about you? Can you help him?"

Fergal shrugged. "Perhaps."

Randolph snorted and dragged Fergal to the wall.

"Fergal," he muttered, his voice low, "I sometimes reckon your claim that your tonic only works on people of good heart is ridiculous, but as it gives most people gut rot, I sometimes reckon it's valid. Either way, a child that young must have a good heart, and if you can do anything . . ."

Fergal nodded and rubbed his hands. "Perhaps I can do something. But I reckon it's time to strike a bargain with Morgana for—"

"That ain't the question I asked." Randolph pushed Fergal back against the wall. He kept him pinned as he stared deep into his eyes. "I've put up with any amount of double-dealing from you, but if you can do something to save that child, just do it without bargaining."

Fergal blinked hard. He tipped back his hat as he looked at Randolph, then nodded.

Randolph released his grip. He patted Fergal's back as he paced by him to stand before Morgana.

Fergal held his hands wide. "Not going well, then?"

"I can't do anything," Morgana whispered. "I don't know about medical matters. I reckon Danny has an . . ."

Morgana sobbed into her hand, then threw back her head as she fought to suppress another sob.

"But your tonic helped Mayor Jack—"

Randolph slammed a hand on Fergal's shoulder.

"Fergal," he muttered, "stop playing games."

Morgana looked at Randolph, then at Fergal.

"What are you two on about?"

Fergal rubbed his shoulder. "We know you didn't really cure Jackson."

"Kent said, but you ain't arguing about that."

"We ain't. I'm offering to help the boy with my tonic."

"We shouldn't insult Gene by pretending to help his child." Morgana lowered her head a moment. A freed tear splashed on the ground. "We both sell a restorative tonic. It perks people up for a while. From what I've heard, yours then makes them ill, whereas mine just tastes good. We do no real harm. But we don't do any real good either."

Fergal shrugged his jacket straight. "Mine is a genuine product."

Morgana provided a wan smile. "You don't need to

convince me. Save your conviction for gullible customers, not for Gene."

"My tonic works." Fergal gestured across the road.
"Come with me."

Fergal turned and scurried off the boardwalk.

Morgana glanced at Randolph, who gave her an encouraging nod, so she dashed after Fergal, through the
crowd, and to his shop.

Fergal scurried inside, grabbed a bottle of tonic, and
held it up to the light. He ripped out the stopper, then
thrust a questing finger in the tonic. Using the tip of
his tongue, he licked the finger and shivered.

He shook his head and dashed back outside, shuffled around Morgana, then into his wagon. He clattered to the back of the wagon, threw open a cabinet,
and grabbed a flask of the recipe.

From his pocket he removed a tube and lowered it
into the flask. He extracted some liquid, then dripped
three large drops of the recipe into his tonic. As he
shook the bottle, the tonic swirled and sparkled to
glow with an even deeper amber than usual.

"Will it work?"

Fergal turned to see Morgana peering through the
door at him.

"If the child is of good heart."

Fergal looked for a reaction, but Morgana just
smiled.

"If we're not exploiting that family, I'll try it."

Fergal locked the cabinet, then paced from his
wagon. He held out a bottle of the stronger tonic.

"You can pour it into your bottle. Gene needn't know that it's my tonic."

Morgana nodded and held the glowing tonic to the sun. Amber light rippled across her face. With a shrug, she poured her tonic on to the ground and refilled it with Fergal's.

They paced back across the road and through the parting crowd. On the boardwalk, Fergal peeled off and joined Randolph, leaving Morgana to enter the saloon alone.

"I saw you letting Morgana pretend your universal remedy is her Lazarus Tonic." Randolph patted Fergal's shoulder. "That was a decent thing to do."

"Wasn't." Fergal rubbed his hands and grinned. "I was hedging my bets in case it fails."

Randolph snorted. He pushed Fergal back a pace, then stormed down the boardwalk and into Warty Bill's to join Morgana.

Fergal edged to the window and looked inside, rubbing his shoulder.

Per Morgana's directions, Randolph held Danny up. Morgana removed the stopper from the tonic bottle and held the rim to the boy's lips.

With an involuntary action, Danny sipped the tonic, then cringed. He then shook his head and cracked open his eyes to glance at the bottle. With his arm slack, he wrapped a hand around the bottle.

Morgana released her grip, but Danny was too weak to hold the bottle and so together, they angled it in. Danny leaned forward six inches and this time he wrapped his lips around the bottle and gulped half of the contents.

Danny opened his eyes a mite more.

"Are you Miss Dempsey?" he said, his voice low.

"I'm not." Morgana glanced at Randolph, then Gene.

Both men nodded back to her.

"Pa says that if I get better, I can go to Miss Dempsey's school."

"You will and you'll enjoy her fine school." Morgana smiled. "I could even fetch her and while you get better, she can start your schooling."

"I'd like that. But I'm tired. Perhaps not now."

Danny's eyes closed and he slumped back. Randolph lowered his hands until he was lying on the table.

Morgana and Gene shared a pained glance.

"But," Danny said, sitting back up. "I reckon I'll have some more of that tonic. It sure perks you up."

Danny snatched the bottle from Morgana's grip and knocked back the remaining contents. He smacked his lips.

"How do you feel?" Morgana asked, her head cocked to one side.

"Fine." Danny glanced around the saloon. "Is this a saloon?"

"It is."

"Horrible, smelly place." He swung his legs to the floor and stretched. "Can I go home now? I don't want to be here."

Morgana staggered back and stood beside Gene.

With their eyes bulging, they watched Danny skip to the door.

"Thank you," Gene said. He grabbed Morgana's hand and shook it again and again. "I can never repay you."

Morgana freed her mangled hand and blew out her cheeks.

"You can by fulfilling his request. Destiny's school needs children."

Gene nodded. "I'll do that."

"Come on, Pa," Danny shouted by the door.

Gene joined his son and, arm in arm, they strode outside. Applause cascaded around them as they winded a path to their cart.

Miss Dempsey edged through the crowd. On bended knee she held Danny's hand and pointed at the school. She received a huge nod and gave an even larger hug in return.

Morgana shook her head, then shuffled up to Randolph.

"Fergal ain't the rogue I took him for," she said.

"He is. But he has a good . . ." Randolph sighed. "A less bad side."

"Tell him that as he didn't try to gain anything for helping that boy, I'll tell him what my recipe is."

"That'll confuse him. The first good deed that scoundrel's ever done got him something that his scheming never could."

"Don't be harsh on him."

Randolph snorted and strode outside.

On the boardwalk, Fergal was watching the cart leave town.

Randolph paced to him and lifted a hand to pat Fergal's shoulder, but he thought he heard Fergal snuffle and lowered his hand.

"Fergal," Randolph whispered. "Were you just . . ."

Fergal stood straight. He smoothed his jacket and turned.

"Just what?" Fergal cleared his throat.

"Nothing." Randolph smiled. "Morgana will give you the recipe for her nice tasting tonic. You got one of the things you wanted—a drinkable tonic."

"Yeah." Fergal glanced at the wagon trundling out of town. "I got one of the things I wanted."

"Come on." Randolph grabbed Fergal's arm and pointed into Warty Bill's. "We got an election to rig."

Chapter Thirteen

With their heads down, Randolph and Fergal snuck into the alley beside Warty Bill's.

They edged through a side window and into the cellar. They huddled, listening to Snide drag the ballot box into the saloon, then to Snide's footfalls as he paced to the door.

In the darkness, they listened to the first ten voters enter the saloon, shuffle to the bar, cast their votes, then leave.

They compared notes as another voter entered and left. Then they counted to five, dashed up the cellar steps, and around the bar.

On the bar, the large tin ballot box sat. Fergal picked the lock and threw the lid open. With their arms whirling, they emptied their pockets of completed ballots.

Even as Randolph hurled the last handful of ballots

146

in, Fergal was slamming the box shut and relocking it. They ducked, nodded to each other, then lunged behind the bar, down the cellar steps, and into the cellar.

The operation took thirty seconds—ten seconds shorter than the time it took for one voter to leave Warty Bill's after casting their vote and the next voter to pass Adam Thornton's less than vigorous vetting procedure at the door.

Silently they edged through the cellar window and down the alley. At the end of the alley, both men leaned on the wall.

Fergal whistled to himself as he read the recipe for Morgana's tonic.

"You reckon that should do it?" Randolph asked, examining his fingernails with a nonchalant gaze.

"We stuffed fifteen ballots apiece. With the ballots I'd hidden in the box before the voting started, that ought to be enough."

"Provided some townsfolk cast a real vote for Sherman."

Both men looked at each other.

"Come on. We'd better stuff some more."

They dashed to Fergal's shop and collected another two handfuls of completed ballots. Then they edged around the outskirts of Destiny and back into Warty Bill's cellar.

They tiptoed across the cellar floor, then, ten paces from the door, footsteps paced down the steps. Both men slid to a halt as a man slipped into the cellar doorway before them.

Randolph snorted as he recognized Kent's outline.

"What you doing here?" Randolph snapped.

Kent flinched, then raised a hand as he peered into the darkness.

"I could ask you the same question," he muttered.

Randolph tapped his star, which gleamed in the light reflected down the cellar steps.

"We're working undercover to ensure that no undesirables get into Warty Bill's and tamper with the election."

Kent glared at Randolph, then at Fergal.

"Reckon as two undesirables have done that already."

"Make that three," Fergal muttered. "But we're Destiny officials. We have a right to be here."

"You ain't officials. You're just some tonic seller and some tonic seller's bodyguard who got it into their heads to better themselves. Not that that takes much doing."

"And what of it?"

"As you ain't real officials, you have no right to do anything official. Or anything unofficial, like stuffing ballots in the ballot box."

"We weren't . . ." Randolph gulped. With as much dignity as he could muster, he thrust his handful of ballots into his pocket.

"But neither have you," Fergal said.

Kent shrugged. "Then, if we both agree that we have no right to be here, we should leave together."

With misplaced pride, each man walked tall through

the darkened cellar and slipped out of Warty Bill's into the alley.

Back on the road, Fergal and Randolph wandered away to stand outside Mrs. Simpson's parlor, and Kent joined Miss Dempsey outside the school, but they still kept each other in their sights.

"Looks like we won't get another chance to stuff ballots," Randolph murmured. "We won't get Sherman elected now."

Fergal shrugged. "I ain't worried."

"You should be. Kent was stuffing the ballot box too."

"He did. But there are two of us." Fergal grinned. "So I reckon we stuffed more ballots than he did."

Two hours after the voting began, Adam gestured for Fergal and the candidates to approach the table outside Warty Bill's.

Adam ran a finger down the list of voters, then smiled.

"All ninety-three voters have cast their votes," he said.

Fergal nodded and turned to face the crowd standing outside Warty Bill's. He held his arms wide.

"I hereby declare the voting closed," he announced.

"Hurrah," everyone shouted.

"Does that mean," Victor shouted, "that Warty Bill's is open?"

"It will be when I've counted the votes."

"Then hurry up. I got a thirst on."

Fergal nodded and turned to Warty Bill's.

"Wait," Jackson muttered, lifting a hand. "You don't expect to count the votes, do you?"

"Yup," Fergal said. "I'm the only official here."

"You ain't an official." Jackson snorted. "I reckon someone needs to ensure that you don't lose any votes."

Fergal sighed. "Sheriff McDougal can come into Warty Bill's and ensure that I don't lose any votes."

Randolph stepped up to join Fergal.

Jackson shook his head. "I'd prefer someone else to be in there who ain't so friendly with you."

"Adam Thornton has vetted the voters before they vote. I suppose that makes him an official too, so he can check that Randolph has ensured that I don't lose any votes."

Adam stood and joined Randolph.

"I was looking for someone even more official than Adam."

Jackson clicked his fingers and Tex strode past him.

Tex raised an eyebrow. "I reckon I can observe Adam checking that Randolph has ensured that Fergal doesn't lose any votes."

Fergal glanced at Tex's gloved right hand. He nodded and Tex joined the line of officials.

Sherman pushed Snide forward. Snide squirmed away, but Sherman grabbed his arm and swung him back.

"And what do you want, Snide?" Fergal asked.

"I don't know," Snide murmured, scratching his forehead.

Sherman sighed. "What Deputy Patterson wants is

to watch Tex observing Adam checking that Randolph has ensured that Fergal doesn't lose any votes. Ain't that so, Snide?"

Snide winced. "Sorry. Can't do that on account of I don't know what you're on about."

Sherman shoved Snide forward. "Just go in there and look official."

With much grumbling, Snide joined the officials.

"Does anybody else," Fergal said, "want to observe anybody else doing anything else?"

"I want to observe you opening Warty Bill's," Victor shouted to a round of applause.

Fergal nodded and led the new officials into Warty Bill's.

Inside, Snide and Tex flanked the bar while Adam, Fergal and Randolph sat on stools at the bar.

Fergal unlocked, then lifted, the lid from the ballot box. He peered inside. With a bemused shake of the head, he poured the ballots on to the bar. A mountain of folded paper grew, and grew.

"Ninety-three ballots sure take up a lot of space," Randolph said, hiding a grin behind his hand.

"They sure do. This might take longer than I thought." Fergal grabbed a handful of ballots that had slipped on to the floor and selected one. He glanced at Randolph. "You ready to ensure that I don't lose any votes?"

"I am," Randolph said.

Fergal turned to Adam. "You ready to check that Randolph ensures that I don't lose any votes?"

"Yeah," Adam said.

Fergal turned to Tex. "You ready to observe Adam checking that Randolph ensures that I don't lose any votes?"

"Yup," Tex grunted.

Fergal turned to Snide. "You ready to watch Tex observing Adam checking that Randolph ensures that I don't lose any votes?"

Snide mouthed his way through this chain of officialdom.

"Nope. I still don't know what's happening."

"Snide," Randolph said, tapping his temple. "A lawman doesn't have to know what's happening. He just has to look as if he knows what's happening." Randolph contemplated Snide and sighed. "But you can just stand at the bar."

Snide grinned, set his feet wide, and leaned back on the bar.

Fergal unfolded the first ballot. He ran his finger down the three candidates' boxes. None of them contained a cross. Fergal frowned and turned the ballot over. Writing was on the other side.

"Fergal O'Brien," he read, "should be run out of town."

Adam scrawled on his note pad. "Check."

"That ain't a vote."

"Reckon as we're seeing democracy in action. People are just using the opportunity to make their feelings heard."

Fergal lifted his eyes to glance at Adam's writing, then glanced at the writing on the ballot.

"Wondered why you took so much time over your voting."

"Elections are anonymous. You got no reason to suppose that was me."

Fergal snorted, scrunched the ballot into a ball, and threw it over his shoulder.

Tex caught the ballot, opened it, and chuckled.

Fergal grabbed the next ballot. It too was blank on the front but not on the back.

Adam peered over Fergal's shoulder and chuckled.

"That ain't one of mine. Are you sure that's how you spell—"

"No." Fergal took a deep breath. "This could take some time."

An hour after the counting began, Fergal emerged from Warty Bill's, closely followed by a line of yawning officials and a head-scratching Snide. He beckoned the candidates to approach, then held his hands wide and faced the expectant and thirsty crowd.

"I now have the election results for the new mayor of Destiny," he announced.

"That mean that Warty Bill's is open?" Victor shouted.

"No."

Victor kicked a stone. "Why is this taking so long?"

"This is taking so long because we all had to observe each other observing each other and because we had a one-hundred percent turnout from the electorate. And such was the enthusiasm for democracy in Destiny that the ninety-three inhabitants cast two hundred and thirty-six votes," Fergal glanced at Adam, "plus some suggestions as to future town policy. I'll ignore those suggestions but read the results in reverse order. In sixth place—"

"But there were only three candidates," Jackson muttered, "and one of them stood down."

Fergal glanced up from his notes. "I don't comment on the validity of the results, I merely relay the facts."

"Well, hurry up. I got a thirst on too."

"In sixth place, with one vote, we have Adam Thornton."

Adam thrust his hands above his head. "Who'd have thought it? Me in sixth place in the race to be mayor."

He bowed in all directions, but in return received nothing but irritated and thirsty stares.

Fergal glared at Adam until he lowered his hands, then faced the crowd.

"In fifth place, with two votes," Fergal sighed and shook his head, "we have X."

"Who in tarnation is X?" Sherman asked.

"Two people added a new candidate to their ballots called X, then put an X beside it. I don't know who . . ." Fergal gazed across the crowd until he reached Snide and Trap, who both had the grace to hang their heads. "Anyhow, in fourth place, with twenty-two votes, we have Kent Sullivan."

Kent paced forward and bowed in all directions.

"Although I didn't request that anyone vote for me," he said, "I'm flattered. If I may take this opportunity—"

"You may not," Fergal snapped. "In third place, with thirty-two votes, we have Colm Jackson."

"Me?" Jackson asked.

"No. Your vote count is still to come."

"But clearly the voters who voted for Colm meant Colin."

"Yeah, I did," Kent shouted, then lowered his head. "Although I don't know what the other thirty-one voters intended."

"There, that's one person who meant me."

Fergal shook his head. "If just one or two people had taken the trouble to write out new ballots on which they'd spelt your name incorrectly, I might agree. But this was a consistent error carried out by many, many people." Fergal glanced at Kent, who was muttering to himself. "So I must conclude that they were referring to a separate person."

"I don't agree, this—"

"Just get on with the announcement," Sherman muttered. "And we'll argue about that later."

"Thank you. In second place, with seventy-two votes, we have Colin Jackson. And in first place, with one hundred and seven votes, we have Blaine Sherman, the new mayor of Destiny."

"Yes!" Sherman shouted, thrusting a fist high into the air.

"I object," Jackson shouted.

"As I've said, the votes cast for Colm Jackson don't count."

"But—"

"And even if you combine the votes cast for Colm Jackson and the votes cast for Colin Jackson," Fergal glanced at his notes, mouthing numbers, "they are still less than the votes cast for Blaine Sherman."

"You're quite right. But I believe the more valid objection is that in a town with only ninety-three inhabitants, Sherman polled one hundred and seven votes."

Fergal gulped. "I see your point. But I don't believe that seventy-two people voted for you."

"I can accept that twenty-one people didn't vote for me. I can't accept that everyone in Destiny, plus fourteen people that don't exist voted for Sherman. I move to declare Sherman's votes invalid and declare me as mayor."

"Your objection is duly noted and duly ignored."

"This is ridiculous. You can't elect a mayor with such a flawed election." Jackson folded his arms. "And someone else agrees with me too."

Tex paced to his side and removed the glove from his right hand, one finger at a time. He glared at Fergal and raised an eyebrow.

"Blatant intimidation won't work." Fergal grabbed his right hand to stop an involuntary tremor. "The electorate has spoken."

Jackson snorted. "And fourteen people that don't exist have spoken too?"

Victor waved an arm above his head. "Perhaps Morgana's Lazarus Tonic has raised some people from the dead and they voted for Sherman."

"That ain't it," Jackson snapped. "Fergal was just mighty keen to stuff that ballot box. We need to hold this election again."

Fergal shook his head. "Why will holding it again get a better result? We had all those watchers and observers and checkers and ensurers and Snide who confirmed that we had proceeded correctly."

"They did no good. You'd already rigged the election. So we do it again and hopefully, you'll have run out of ballots to stuff in that ballot box."

Fergal shrugged. "All right. We'll hold the election again."

Jackson eyed Fergal's firm jaw. He nodded.

"And in case you haven't run out of ballots to stuff, we'll vote in triplicate. Each candidate will guard their own box and the election is only valid if all three boxes agree."

"And if they don't?"

Jackson slammed a fist down on his open palm. "We vote again and we keep on voting until we have something we *can* agree on."

"That could take all day."

"It'll take all week," Randolph whispered to himself, "to stuff that many ballot boxes."

For long moments Fergal and Jackson glared at each other, but at the back of the crowd, Bob was whispering to Miss Dempsey.

She nodded. "That could work. Come with me Mr. Bob."

Miss Dempsey edged through the throng with Bob at her heels.

"What do you want?" Fergal asked, turning from Jackson.

"I want to offer a better solution," she said, stepping

onto the boardwalk. She drew her shawl around her shoulders and stared at Fergal, then at Jackson over her half-glasses. "As you *men* don't know how to hold a fair election, you need impartial citizens such as myself and Mr. Bob to apply rigorous procedures to the voting and to declare the right winner, whoever that should be."

She held a hand out and Bob paced on to the boardwalk to join her.

"Ain't that whomever?" Bob asked from the corner of his mouth.

Miss Dempsey glanced at Bob. "You mean—isn't that whomever?"

"Sorry. Isn't that whomever?"

"No. Don't overreach yourself."

Chapter Fourteen

Fifty minutes into the second—and the first uncorrupted—election, Randolph edged to the front of the line of voters.

At the entrance to the school Tex was standing guard. He opened his jacket to reveal his star, then tapped Jackson's badge.

Randolph snorted. "I assume in my case, the slogan is, 'Vote for Colin Jackson or I'll take your job.' "

"Nope," Tex muttered. "I'll be sheriff no matter what you do. But if you don't vote the right way, you'll lose your job and your life."

Randolph shrugged and strode past Tex into the school.

Miss Dempsey and Bob sat at a desk. Beside them the ballot box stood on a table. In the corner a curtained cubicle was the only other furniture.

She looked up. "Name?"

159

"It's me."

"Name?"

Randolph sighed. "Randolph McDougal."

She whispered to Bob.

Bob nodded. "Yup. That's him."

"Of course it's me," Randolph said. "You see me every day."

Miss Dempsey peered at Randolph over her half-glasses.

"We're conducting this election using the strictest of procedures." Miss Dempsey lifted a ballot off a pile of clean ballots, wrote '43' on it, then held it before Bob. "The result will be the fairest possible."

Randolph glanced over his shoulder to see Tex's shadow darkening the doorway. Randolph couldn't tell for sure but Tex appeared to be clutching Victor's throat while he held him two feet off the ground and shook him.

"Forty-three, Miss Dempsey." Bob leaned over a sheet of paper and with his tongue protruding, wrote Randolph's name.

Randolph lifted on his heels to see that some of the letters were even right.

She pointed to the cubicle. "You have one minute to cast your vote in the cubicle, then return to the ballot box and sign it."

Randolph sauntered into the cubicle. He drew the curtain, scrawled an X in Sherman's box, then tapped the wall, but received a solid sound. He knelt and kicked the floorboards, but they provided a solid sound too. The roof was twenty feet above his head. The curtain was eight feet high. He leaned against the wall and peered in all directions, but couldn't see how to sneak into the curtained area without Miss Dempsey and Bob seeing him.

His minute of voting ended and still lacking an idea, he drew back the curtain, signed his ballot at the table, then slipped it in the box. He tipped his hat, then sauntered outside to join Fergal, who was ten men down the queue.

"Miss Dempsey's conducting the election in a more thorough way than we did," he said.

Fergal chuckled. "That ain't difficult. What's the weakness?"

"Her procedures are perfect. I reckon we have to let democracy take its course."

"Very funny. What's she doing that's so perfect?"

"The ballot box is in the center of the room and every ballot gets a number. You sign on the back and Bob keeps a separate record of the number and your name. Even if we could get to the ballot box, no amount of stuffing it with ballots will help if the signatures, the numbers, and the names on Bob's record don't match."

"And there lies the flaw."

Randolph considered Fergal a moment, then shrugged.

"I don't get what—"

"Don't worry. Just find Snide and tell him to cause a diversion in fifteen minutes."

As Randolph dashed away, Fergal paced forward in

the line. From the corner of his eye, he saw Kent standing outside Warty Bill's.

As the next nervous voter edged past the glowering Tex and into the school, Kent scrawled a note on a sheet of paper. Fergal watched, and when the next voter slipped inside, Kent scrawled again. Then Kent wandered across the road.

Fergal rocked back and forth a moment, then sauntered from the line to follow Kent.

With a last glance along the road, Kent slipped into his wagon.

Fergal scurried to the side of the wagon.

Ten minutes later Kent emerged. A coil of rope dangled from his shoulder. A hammer protruded from his pocket.

"What are you doing?" Fergal muttered.

Kent flinched and turned. He sneered. "I don't need to explain myself."

"You noted the names and positions in the queue of the voters and you've forged their signatures on fresh ballots."

Kent snorted. "I assume you know that because you had the same plan?"

"Yup. But you've forgotten the diversion so you can get the ballots in the ballot box."

"I haven't. I've paid Trap to cause one."

Fergal sighed. Through narrowed eyes, he considered Kent.

"This ain't doing either of us any good."

"I ain't interested in a deal." Kent snorted. "I'll find a way that you ain't considered."

Kent shook a fist at Fergal, but a ballot fluttered from his sleeve. He lunged for the ballot, but Fergal grabbed it, Kent's hand closing on air.

Fergal glanced at the ballot, then furrowed his brow.

"This ballot votes for you." Fergal pointed at the cross beside Kent Sullivan's name. "You've told your supporters to vote for Jackson, but you're still trying to win."

"I had no choice." Kent's shoulders slumped. "For me, Jackson's election slogan was, 'Tell your supporters to change their votes or Tex will rip your head off.' "

"You're taking a big risk." Fergal leaned to Kent and held his hands wide. "Just how badly do you want to become mayor?"

After another hour of voting, and twenty minutes of counting, Miss Dempsey and Bob emerged onto the boardwalk outside the school.

In her right hand Miss Dempsey clutched a single sheet of paper. She gestured for the candidates to join her, then cleared her throat and faced the assembled crowd.

"I have the result," she announced, "of the second, and valid, election."

"Does that mean . . ." Victor lowered his head when she glared at him over the top of her half-glasses.

"The ninety-three voters of Destiny cast ninety-two valid votes. Only one ballot was spoilt with the casting of a vote for an ineligible candidate." She glared at Adam.

"But I was sixth last time," Adam muttered. "That just ain't fair."

"If you wished your vote to be valid, you should have stood for mayor." She glanced at her notes. "The votes are as follows: Mr. Sullivan has one vote. Mr. Sherman has twenty-two votes. Mr. Jackson has sixty-nine votes. I hereby declare that Mr. Jackson is the new mayor of Destiny."

"Yes!" Jackson thrust his hands above his head. Then, remembering his fake wound, lowered his hands and rubbed his chest.

"I protest," Sherman muttered.

"On what grounds?" Miss Dempsey asked.

Sherman glanced around and sighed. "As soon as I find my campaign manager, I'll present plenty of grounds."

Chapter Fifteen

Sherman glared up and down the road, but his gaze came to rest on Fergal, who was edging into the school. Sherman stormed in after him to find Fergal skulking behind a desk.

"You promised me I'd become mayor," Sherman muttered and advanced a long pace on Fergal, but Fergal merely shrugged his jacket and stood his ground.

Sherman glanced away, then stormed round the desk and smashed a round-armed punch into Fergal's jaw, sending him reeling. Even as Fergal skidded to a halt, Sherman loomed over him and grabbed his collar. He hoisted him from the floor and drew back his fist.

"Don't hit me," Fergal screeched and ripped a scroll and envelope from his pocket. He held out the envelope.

Sherman released Fergal's collar. As Fergal clattered to the floor, he snatched the envelope from his hand and backed a pace, ripping it open.

"So you've given me the bonds, but I still need a valid objection so I can be mayor."

Sherman stood over Fergal again and pulled back his fist.

Fergal cringed from a blow that didn't come. He coughed to regain his composure.

"You don't want to be mayor." Fergal held out one of the scrolls that Miss Dempsey and Adam Thornton had signed two days ago. "You just want proof that you're entitled to act on Destiny's behalf."

Sherman unfurled the scroll and read it, but his sneer stayed.

"Forgeries won't get me the money."

"This is no forgery. You *were* the mayor of Destiny—for about two seconds. Then Jackson objected. But for those two seconds you were Mayor Blaine Sherman of Destiny."

Sherman rolled up the scroll. "I suppose I was."

"And you have the papers to prove it."

"This could work." Sherman rubbed the scroll against his chin. "It looks official."

"That's because it is." Fergal rolled to his haunches, he rubbed his jaw, then stood tall. "It's signed by Miss Dempsey, Adam Thornton and me—three people beyond reproach."

Sherman nodded. "One out of three should do it."

"And it'll work even better than if you were the real mayor." Fergal laid a friendly hand on Sherman's shoulder. "The townsfolk won't care about you leaving and won't realize you disappeared with Destiny's funds."

Sherman shrugged Fergal's hand from him. He shoved the scroll and the envelope in his inside pocket, then gave Fergal a begrudging nod and strode outside. With a firm pace, he strode up to Jackson.

"Are you contesting the election?" Jackson asked.

"Nope. I hereby concede and withdraw." Sherman held out a hand. "I acknowledge you as the mayor of Destiny."

"Yes," Jackson cried and again thrust his arms into the air in celebration.

Stony silence greeted him.

Jackson lowered his arms, rubbed his chest, and gave Sherman's hand a slight shake, then gave a subdued wave to the crowd.

Sherman slunk to his horse, his head low but with his eyes still bright. With a last look around the town, and a nod to Fergal in the school doorway, he mounted his horse and cantered out of town.

"Does that mean," Victor muttered, "that Warty Bill's is open?"

Jackson glanced around, but on receiving nothing but enthusiastic nods, he nodded.

A cheer sounded. Hurled hats rained down as everyone dashed into Warty Bill's, pushing and shoving in their eagerness to reach the bar.

Jackson shrugged, then filed into the saloon after them.

When the road cleared, only Snide and Trap remained. They rolled over and over as they fought in the middle of the road.

Fergal wandered down the boardwalk to Randolph's side.

"Why are they fighting?" he asked.

Randolph sighed. "I reckon that's the diversion just starting up."

Randolph left Fergal to wander into Warty Bill's and, with several well-placed kicks, encouraged Snide to stop his diverting behavior. Together they sauntered towards Warty Bill's, but as the saloon was heaving and bustling, they headed to the sheriff's office instead.

In the doorway, both men skidded to a halt.

Tex Porter was leaning back behind the desk, smoking a cigar.

"What you doing here?" Randolph muttered.

"Enjoying the ambience in my office." Tex blew out a smoke circle.

"You ain't the sheriff here."

"Unless you didn't notice, Jackson is now the mayor of Destiny."

"I noticed." Randolph paced into the office. "But however tough you act, you wouldn't kill two lawmen."

"That's one lawman and an idiot."

Snide threw back his head and roared with laughter.

Randolph slapped Snide's shoulder. "He means I'm the lawman, Snide."

Snide's laughter died and he hung his head.

"I do," Tex muttered. He placed the cigar on the

edge of the desk and stood. He removed his glove, one finger at a time, and paced round the desk to face Randolph. "And you're right. I wouldn't kill a lawman. The risk is too great. But I would run one out of town."

Tex glanced away, then thundered a blow into Randolph's jaw, sending him sprawling. He stared at Randolph's prone form a moment, confirming he was out cold, then snapped round to face Snide.

"But as for you," he muttered.

Snide gulped. "Leave town or die?"

"Nope. You just die."

Snide scrambled for his gun, but Tex slammed a hand on his arm, the grip like iron. He pulled Snide's arm up, then slipped the gun from Snide's holster with his other hand and tossed it into the corner of the office.

"What you going to do?" Snide babbled.

Tex grinned. "See those cell bars?"

Snide glanced over his shoulder. "Yup."

"See that hammer?"

"Yup."

"See your arms and legs?"

"Yup."

Tex raised his eyebrows. "Can you not see where I'm going with this?"

Snide gulped. "Unfortunately I can. That's the trouble with getting schooled. You get a better imagination."

"And you're right." Tex twisted Snide's arm up his

back and marched him to the central cell. "Prepare to get wrapped round these cell bars."

"Wait!"

Tex slammed Snide into the bars. "For what?"

"To bargain. You're a hired gun. For the right price I can hire you."

"You can." Tex set his feet wide. "But I reckon what you can offer on your deputy's wage won't match what Jackson pays me."

"Whatever it is," Snide babbled, "I'll double it."

"That's a mighty big number. Want to guess what it is?" Tex placed his mouth beside Snide's ear and lowered his voice. "I'll give you a clue. It's so big I reckon you can't even count that high."

"Ten dollars?"

"Nope." Tex hoisted Snide's arm up, forcing him on to tiptoes. "You'll have to do better than that."

"Twenty thousand then," Snide shrieked.

Tex released Snide for him to crash to the floor.

"You just got my attention. Where can you get your hands on that sort of money?"

Snide rolled round to face Tex. "I can't. But you can. It's heading to Clementine at a gallop right now."

Tex rubbed his chin. "Sherman?"

Snide nodded frantically. "You got it."

Randolph opened his eyes. As his vision focused he flexed his jaw. Standing over him were Snide and Fergal. He closed his eyes a moment.

"Where's Tex?" he murmured.

"I saw him off," Snide said, hoisting his gunbelt higher.

Randolph rubbed his eyes, then his jaw.

"Tex must have hit me pretty hard. I thought you just said that you saw Tex off."

"I did. Miss Dempsey has schooled me. And that was a good chance to use that schooling." Snide patted his temple. "So I out-thought him. And sent him after Sherman."

"I never thought I'd say this, but . . ." Randolph took a deep breath. "You've earned my respect, Deputy."

"Obliged." Snide grinned and swaggered to the door.

Randolph let Fergal drag him to his feet. The two men followed Snide outside and down the boardwalk.

"You surprised at Snide?" Randolph asked.

"No. Two days ago, I planted the idea in his mind as to how he could defeat Tex." Fergal smiled as Snide wandered into Warty Bill's. "Guess Miss Dempsey's schooling encouraged it to burrow its way out."

"That makes things clearer. Snide out-thinking anyone just didn't seem right." Randolph stopped on the boardwalk and faced Fergal. "Are you heading to Clementine too?"

"Nope." Fergal chuckled. "Tex will catch Sherman soon and if anything is left afterwards, I don't fancy being around."

"You double-crossed Sherman before he paid you. And Tex will get the money. That wasn't clever."

"I double-crossed Sherman before he double-crossed me." Fergal cupped a hand beside his mouth and leaned to Randolph. "And I sent word to Marshal Vermain that the wrong person will arrive at the offices of Sweeney, Sweeney, Sweeney and Carter to collect the money. With any luck, some lawyers might get caught in the crossfire."

Fergal shrugged his jacket straight and sauntered into the saloon.

Inside Warty Bill's, Jackson was holding court by the bar. He was smiling broadly and gesticulating to Bob, Kent, and Miss Dempsey.

"So, Kent," Jackson said, "this is my town now."

Kent patted Jackson's back. "And for your first act, I assume you'll offer your support to Miss Dempsey's school for gunslingers?"

"I'll support it—just like I promised. If Tex arrests a troublemaker, they can go to the school instead of going to the jail." Jackson licked his lips. "Of course, if any of them should die during the arrest, they won't."

Kent's smile died as he contemplated Jackson's sly grin.

"You can't do that," Bob muttered, flexing a fist as he pushed by Kent to face up to Jackson.

"Mr. Bob," Miss Dempsey said. "Remember the skills I've taught you."

"I have." Bob tipped his hat. "I was about to tell our mayor that last week, I'd have knocked him through a window for such double-crossing. But today, I won't. And that ought to prove the good you're doing."

Jackson snorted. "But that's irrelevant, because no-body is stopping me and Tex from doing exactly what we want to do in my town."

Jackson glanced over Kent's shoulder. Roger Thackery was sauntering to the bar. He pulled a pencil from behind his ear and scrawled on a pad.

"Congratulations, Mr. Mayor," he said. "It's time to pay up."

"For what?"

"For one school duly built, and for one jail duly built. All in double-quick time and at double-pay rates." Roger flashed his pad at Jackson.

Jackson gulped. "That's a lot of noughts. But it doesn't matter to me. Sherman ordered those buildings."

"The mayor ordered them. Are you the mayor?"

"Yes, but—"

"Dale," Roger called outside, "get Big Mike. Customer ain't paying."

"I didn't say that," Jackson shouted, raising his arms. "I didn't order the school or the jail."

"Sounds like not paying to me." Roger narrowed his eyes. "Has Destiny got a hospital?"

"No. You offering to build one?"

"Nope, just asking."

Jackson shrugged his jacket and squared up to Roger.

"Does this gesture mean anything to you?" Jackson mimed removing a glove from his right hand, one finger at a time.

"Yup. Tex Porter does that before he hurts people."

Roger grinned. "Although as Tex just galloped out of Destiny like the Devil himself was on his tail, he won't be removing any gloves for a while around here. Do you still want me to fetch Big Mike?"

Jackson gulped. "The mayor owes you all that money, right?"

"Yup."

Jackson glanced around Warty Bill's. He snorted.

"Then I'll resign as mayor. I never understood the attraction of running this festering trash heap anyway. Someone else can deal with this."

Jackson shrugged his jacket closed and strode to the door, brushing past Fergal. He kicked one of the swinging doors to the floor, then strode outside.

As Jackson leapt on his horse and headed out of town, Fergal patted Roger's back, then grabbed Kent's arm and thrust it high.

"As Sherman withdrew from the election," he shouted, "I hereby declare that the third placed candidate is mayor—Kent Sullivan."

"Hey," Adam whined, stepping up to the bar. "He only got one vote, his own, just like me."

"But you weren't a candidate. If you were, it'd have been a tie." Fergal leaned to Adam and chuckled. "And as standing mayor I'd have had the casting vote. And I hate Kent Sullivan more than I hate you."

"That just ain't fair," Adam whined.

"So, you're the new mayor," Roger said, thrusting his pad to Kent.

Kent nodded and glanced at the pad. He gulped.

Chapter Sixteen

From the bar, Randolph and Fergal watched Kent bluster and gesticulate to Roger until Miss Dempsey joined in the debate.

Randolph moved toward her, but Fergal pulled him back.

"Leave her to it," Fergal said. "She's a good negotiator."

Within seconds, Miss Dempsey and Roger were shaking hands. Then Roger thrust his pad under his arm and strode outside, whistling.

Kent took Miss Dempsey's arm and pointed to a free table in the corner of the saloon.

"She is." Randolph sighed. "But couldn't you have found an objection to Kent becoming mayor?"

"No. I told Roger to demand money from Jackson so he'd resign and I could declare Kent as mayor."

"You got my rival elected," Randolph spluttered.

"I did." Fergal grinned. "In return for his memorabilia exhibition. Now I can earn a living as a showman while I'm redesigning my universal—"

"I was more concerned with you supporting my rival."

"I did it for you. It forces you to act. You have to punch Kent now before it's too late. Then all your problems will be over. But do the more important thing." Fergal straightened Randolph's jacket, polished his star, and pointed him towards Miss Dempsey. "Tell her what you think of her."

Randolph gritted his teeth and turned from Fergal. He edged back and forth, but Fergal shoved him forward a pace. Randolph wheeled to a halt. He glanced back at Fergal, received a smile, then took a deep breath and strode across the saloon to her side. He coughed.

"So, Miss Dempsey."

"Yes," she said, unhooking her arm from Kent's arm.

Randolph sighed. "Did you sort out Roger?"

"I persuaded him to see sense."

"Good." Randolph rocked from foot to foot. Kent was glaring at him, so he stood sideways to Kent and smiled. "I was . . . I was wondering . . ."

Miss Dempsey turned to Kent. "Mr. Sullivan, please secure our table."

Kent narrowed his eyes and edged towards Randolph, but on Miss Dempsey's blind side Randolph shook a fist at him. Kent snorted and headed for the table.

"So, Miss Dempsey, I was . . ." Randolph gulped. "You talked to Gene about schooling his son."

"I did. Danny is a charming boy. And as soon as he recovers from his stomachache, I'll school him, and then I'll have fulfilled my dream." She smiled and faced Randolph. "One child is all I need. Plus one adult and Deputy Patterson."

"And you know who you have to thank for that?" Randolph stood tall and puffed his chest.

"I do." She glanced at Kent, who was now sitting. "Mr. Sullivan is marvelous, but Miss Sullivan is a positive treasure."

"Miss Sullivan!" Randolph clenched his hands into tight fists. "It just ain't fair. Morgana's tonic didn't save Danny's life. Fergal's tonic did."

"I know."

"And Kent . . . Pardon?"

"I know. Miss Sullivan told me about Mr. O'Brien's marvelous gesture."

"Then why do you reckon she helped the school?"

"I explained my problem to her, so for the last two days she has ignored her stall and scoured the countryside for a family that I can teach in my school. And she found the Thompson family."

Randolph shrugged. "I didn't know that."

"I fear you've misunderstood Miss Sullivan. I'd hoped you could get on. The decent people in Destiny should." She sighed. "And it's such a pity that we can't all sit down for dinner now and resolve your differences."

"It is." Randolph slumped. "I'll go."

"It isn't that. You're welcome to eat with us. But Miss Sullivan has left town." Miss Dempsey raised her eyebrows. "But there was something that you were wondering about."

"I was wondering . . ." Randolph hung his head a moment, then slapped his forehead. "Forget it."

He tipped his hat and dashed to the bar. On the run, he grabbed Fergal's elbow and dragged him outside.

"Did you tell her?" Fergal asked.

"Forget that. Just answer this—has everyone got what they wanted?"

"Sort of. Jackson hasn't. I have. Kent, Sherman and Tex have—for now. And you will have soon."

"And did Morgana get what she wanted?"

"I don't know." Fergal shrugged. "What you getting at?"

Randolph turned to glare into Warty Bill's and snorted.

"According to Miss Dempsey, Morgana already knew the child you cured."

"She what?" Fergal glared into Warty Bill's.

"No point looking for her in there." Randolph pointed across the road. "Apparently, she left town."

Fergal and Randolph turned to glare across the road, then Fergal dashed from the boardwalk, Randolph two paces behind.

Before the remnants of the stable, they skidded to a halt. Kent's wagon was gone, but abandoned in a huge pile beside the stable were cabinets and crates—Kent's exhibition of authentic historical memorabilia.

Fergal lifted crates and rummaged through cabinets,

then rocked back on his heels. He winced, then dashed to his shop. Randolph hurtled after him, reaching the shop as Fergal emerged from his wagon, his head hung.

Randolph glanced over Fergal's shoulder into the wagon. At the back, the cupboard doors were open and rocking back and forth. The flasks of tonic weren't inside.

"Morgana's stolen my recipe," Fergal whined.

Randolph sighed and patted his shoulder.

"I'm sorry for you, but you're just as big a double-crosser as she is. All the time you were scamming her for the secret of her tonic, she was scamming you for the secret of yours. Perhaps she is your half-sister. You ought to be proud."

"I ain't. She's worse than me. She used a child."

"But you probably got Sherman and Tex killed. You can't profess superior morals."

"I can. Those men deserve to have their bad intentions turned against them. But she used my better side to steal my tonic. And people who turn good intentions against their victims have no right to sell my universal remedy."

Randolph nodded. He slammed a fist into his other palm and turned.

"You're right. And I'm just riled enough now to punch the other half of the Sullivan family."

"Randolph," Fergal shouted.

Randolph turned back. "Yeah?"

Fergal smiled. "Just knock Kent through a few windows and do right by Miss Dempsey."

Randolph nodded and strode across the road to Warty Bill's. He pushed open the remaining swing door and stood holding on to it. Inside, Miss Dempsey and Kent were chatting at their table. Blood thundered in Randolph's ears.

"You're a two-bit scoundrel, Kent," he roared.

Saloon talk died as Kent jumped to his feet.

"I won't stand for that."

"Then sit down, because I have a lot more to say to you." Randolph pushed back the swinging door and stalked across the saloon. He squared off to Kent. "Do you know what this man has been doing, Miss Dempsey?"

She stood. "He's supported me while he became mayor."

"Wrong. He colluded with Jackson to pretend Jackson had been shot. He colluded with everyone to rig the election. He colluded with Morgana to steal Fergal's tonic. He has an exhibition full of fraudulent memorabilia he makes in his wagon. He has . . . He has . . . He has all that and that's just the start of what's wrong with him."

"Sheriff McDougal, is that the worst you can accuse him of doing? Because based on the actions of everybody else in Destiny, that makes him a saint."

"There is something worse." Randolph hitched himself to his full height. "He ain't good enough for you. You deserve more than a cheap huckster."

"Who I spend my evenings with is not your concern."

"It is. Because you deserve me." Randolph gulped,

his cheeks warming, but he puffed his chest with pride. "There. I've said it. He ain't good enough for you. I am."

Miss Dempsey opened and closed her mouth silently, but Kent stood before Randolph.

"I won't accept that," Kent said. "You, sir, are no gentleman."

"And neither are you. You're just a cheap huckster."

"And you're just a cheap huckster's bodyguard."

"Fergal ain't cheap!"

With blood pounding in his ears, Randolph advanced a pace on Kent. He fought to control his breathing, but his chest tightened. He swung back his fist and with a long, round-armed punch, slugged Kent's jaw.

Kent lifted off the floor before he crashed on his back.

Miss Dempsey squealed and knelt at Kent's side, but Randolph continued to advance.

Snide and Bob dashed from the bar to stand before Randolph.

"Violence ain't the way," Bob said. "You and Kent can talk out your problems."

Randolph snorted and pushed him aside. Snide still blocked his way.

"Surely you ain't saying that banging heads is wrong?" Randolph snapped.

"No. It's fine as a last resort." Snide tapped his forehead. "But you think first."

Randolph sneered and pushed Snide to the side. He

stood over Kent, but Miss Dempsey jumped to her feet and glared at him, her eyes blazing.

"You're a cheap huckster's bodyguard? Does Mayor Sullivan mean Mr. O'Brien?"

Randolph gulped. "He does. But he's no cheap huckster."

"I know. Mr. O'Brien is a man of integrity." Miss Dempsey grabbed an envelope from the table and waved it at Randolph. "He gave me these bonds."

Randolph slapped his forehead. "Sherman is heading to Clementine with a forged copy of the bonds."

"I don't know about that, but he said that the offices of Sweeney, Sweeney, Sweeney and Carter will fill the town's coffers next week. And in return for delaying payment on the school and jail, I've already allocated the rebuilding work for the rest of Destiny to Mr. Thackery."

Randolph glared at Kent. "Unless *he* steals the money first."

Kent rubbed his brow and sat up. "I won't."

Randolph rolled his shoulders and moved to pass Miss Dempsey, but she held her hands wide, blocking him.

"Don't hit him."

"Because it ain't seemly for a mayor and sheriff to brawl in a saloon?"

"It isn't."

"No problem." Randolph stormed round Miss Dempsey towards Kent. "Because he's just a cheap huckster and I'm just a huckster's bodyguard."

On his back, Kent wheeled away from Randolph,

but Miss Dempsey slapped Randolph's shoulder, halting him.

"Get out, Randolph," she screamed. "Just get out!"

Randolph merely shrugged and bunched a fist.

On the floor, Kent held his jaw and lay back, closing his eyes as he exaggerated his pain.

Randolph threw back his fist, but Snide grabbed his arm and Bob grabbed his other arm. They dragged him back a pace. Randolph struggled, but they gripped his arms more tightly and marched him across the saloon, through the door, and onto the boardwalk.

"Reckon you didn't handle that well," Bob said, releasing Randolph's arm.

Randolph glared into Warty Bill's, but as the tightness in his chest and the blood pounding in his ears receded, he nodded.

He patted the other mens' shoulders, then turned to look into the road. It was deserted. Kent's exhibition had gone, but so had Fergal's wagon, the remnants of his shop lying in a wrecked heap.

For long moments Randolph hung his head, then dashed across the road to find the spot where the wheel tracks started. They rolled out of town, heading north, presumably joining Morgana's wagon tracks. He put a hand to his brow and peered up the nearest hill, but he couldn't see Fergal's wagon.

"Fergal's gone," Snide said, as he sidled up to him. "You going too?"

Randolph sighed, then nodded. "Yup."

"Are you returning?"

Randolph glanced at Warty Bill's. Miss Dempsey

was looking through the window at him. Then she turned away and helped Kent to sit behind a table.

"I don't know. Why do you want to know?"

"I've been a deputy for a week. What with seeing off Tex, and what with those lessons that Miss Dempsey's been giving me, I reckon I'm ready for more responsibility."

"And as Sherman's left, he won't make you sheriff."

Snide gulped. "How did you know that?"

"Snide, you're an untrustworthy, violent, worthless varmint." Randolph unhooked his star and pinned it on Snide's chest. "So, yeah, you'll make a good sheriff of Destiny."

"Obliged." Snide scratched his head. "Hey, I ain't untrustworthy."

"You're right. I'm sorry." As Fergal had rigged Randolph's horse to his wagon, he paced to Snide's horse and mounted it. "I'll leave your horse in New Utopia for you to collect. But just do two things for me. Look out for Miss Dempsey, and keep going to her school. Destiny won't always be like it is now. One day soon it'll need a sheriff with some skills."

"I'll do that. And don't let Kent worry you. She'll realize he's no good before too long. And I can put in a bad word or two about him for you." Snide smiled. "And if you want, I can bang his head against the wall."

"What happened to thinking first?"

"I *have* thought, and I reckon that man needs his head banged."

"You're a lawman. You can't . . ." Randolph sighed. "You're a lawman. You can do anything you want."

"Great. I'll get Trap to do that." Snide furrowed his brow. "In case anyone asks, why are you leaving?"

"I have to help Fergal retrieve a tonic recipe from Morgana Sullivan to stop her abusing it."

Snide scratched his head. "I don't understand."

Randolph laughed. "For once, we agree. I don't know why either."

"But a lawman doesn't need to know what's happening." Snide tapped his temple. "He just has to look as if he knows what's happening."

"I'm not a lawman now. I'm just a huckster's bodyguard."

"Ain't no difference other than the number of people you look after."

Randolph nodded. "You're a wise man, Snide."

Snide grinned wildly and tipped his hat, knocking it to the ground. As he bent to grab it, Randolph tipped his hat and galloped out of Destiny, heading north.

With each stride, the urge to look back grew, so at the top of the first hill, he pulled his horse to a halt and looked down toward Destiny.

He saw only two people on the road—Snide and Trap. Snide was standing on the boardwalk outside Adam's hotel, miming banging two large objects together to Trap. Then Trap scurried into Warty Bill's, while Snide swaggered into the sheriff's office.

Randolph glanced at the school for the last time, then turned his horse and put a hand to his brow. Halfway up the next hill a wagon was trundling away.

Randolph sighed, then sat tall in the saddle and galloped after Fergal.